DEVIL
IN THE BEDROOM

JP STORM

Devil In The Bedroom by JP Storm

ISBN 978-1-952027-62-8 (Paperback)
ISBN 978-1-952027-63-5 (Hardback)
ISBN 978-1-952027-64-2 (eBook)

This book is written to provide information and motivation to readers. Its purpose is not to render any type of psychological, legal, or professional advice of any kind. The content is the sole opinion and expression of the author, and not necessarily that of the publisher.

Printed in the United States of America.

New Leaf Media, LLC
175 S. 3rd Street, Suite 200
Columbus, OH 43215
www.thenewleafmedia.com

The story you're about to
read actually happen.

Only the names were change.

Jpstorm2015@yahoo.com

PREFACE

I WAS AWAKENED by a faint scream of "Momm…mie" so I sat up in bed and heard it again "Momm…mie." I ran up the stairs and was shocked by what I was seeing.

I couldn't believe that could be my child laying on the floor with her head bobbing up and down.

I kept thinking where is all that black stuff coming from, not realizing it was blood. I must have stood there for a minute or two but it seems like hours had pass as I watch Dillon continue to strike Sky and with each blow her head would come up off the floor and back down.

As if in a dream like state, I snapped out of it and realize this was no dream – he was killing my child.

I screamed at him "**Stop hitting her**, **get off her** and **leave my house!**" He slowly turns around, looks at me and said in a calm voice, "Oh so where am I supposed to go?" I replied, "I don't care but you have to get out now."

Dillon started walking away and half way down the hall he turns around and comes back into the room. As I was kneeling down to check on my daughter, he grabs me from behind, throws me behind Sky, which cause me to break the mirrored closet door.

I remembered I bounced from the shattered glass of the closet and hitting my head on the edge of the night stand. I could hear Sky quietly saying, "Stop! Don't hurt my mom."

Once I realize she was coherent, I gently nudge her with my foot and said, "Run if you can and don't look back. I'll be ok. I'll find you."

I looked up and saw him coming, stepping over Sky and around the bed with a ceramic lamp, wrapping the cord around the base. I was thinking what is he doing... the bulb is still in there. As Sky begin to crawl away, he leaned down and hit me with the base of the lamp.

He kept hitting me saying "I'm not going anywhere." He kept hitting me till the base of the lamp shattered. He took the part of the base with the bulb and struck me with it till the bulb broke. At that moment I realize I could no longer see out my left eye.

I'm getting ahead of myself so let me start at the beginning of how Sky and Dillon came to be

CHAPTER ONE

SKY WAS A beautiful young black woman of Indian decent with long black flowing hair, fair complexion and piercing black eyes.

On this particular hot day, she had on a white and navy-blue summer dress, matching heels, hat and gloves. The way she would dress caused people to stop and stare as her attire was from the fifty and sixty era which was her signature look.

She was dating her best friend Jasper, a handsome young man that I knew for sure was the one. They appeared so much in love … that is until Dillon came along.

She had just finish visiting with friends in the Crenshaw area and was standing at the corner waiting for the light to change when a black stretch limo drove up and stop.

As she was crossing the street, she heard someone yelling "Hey you! Hey you!" Sky kept walking thinking to herself he couldn't be talking to me. When the light changed the limo made a U-turn and came upon the side of the street where her car was parked.

As she unlocked the car door, a man got out of the driver side of the limo and opens the back door.

According to Sky, out steps the most handsome man she had ever seen. He was tall, very well dressed and groomed. His skin was the color of honey and wore sun glasses that cost more than what she made in a month. His hair was midnight black and when he opened his mouth to speak, she knew was hooked.

He stood there in the glistening sun with a beautiful smile, took off his sun glasses and had the most beautiful piercing blue/green eyes. He held out his hand and introduced himself as Dillon Mason.

She tilted her head to look up at him. With a smile in her voice placed her hand in his and replied, "My name is Skylar Grant," and with that being said he bent to kiss her hand.

Still holding her hand, he said, "That's a beautiful name for a beautiful and stunning young woman. If you're not busy, I would love to take you to lunch and bring you back to your car afterwards."

She was smitten by his good looks, limo, chauffer, the smell of success with a capital S and followed him to the limo.

They had lunch which turned into dinner. After dinner they were driven around Beverly Hills then to Bel Air to look at the sights. Later to Malibu for drinks and to watch the waves. During that evening he told her he was single and lived in Beverly Hills in the family estate.

Before taking Sky back to her car, he ordered his driver Gage, to take him to his storage.

When Gage got to the gate, he used a remote to open the doors... all thirteen of them. Behind twelve of the doors was a car and behind door thirteen was a private plane. All the cars were very expensive and in dark colors - all but one. It was the color of a red tomato. A two seated Jaguar, the car of her dreams. And there it was right in front of her. She squealed with delight like a kid in a candy store as she got closer and closer to the Jaguar.

Sky learned later Dillon owned the storage facility and everything in it. This storage was only used to houses his cars and private plane. (At least that's what he told her).

This was all new to Sky as she had never seen or experienced anything of this magnitude. She was wondering if a man, one man could possibly own all this.

She stood in the storage facility in total awe and for the first time in her life was completely speechless.

She later told me all the cars looked as though they had been washed and polish, as if they were show cars on display. He gave her a tour and begin telling her what type of cars they were. She had only heard and or seen cars like that in magazines or Auto Shows.

But to be here and this close to all those expensive cars made her feel as though she was dreaming and yet there she stood with Dillon Mason. The owner of twelve cars including her dream car and a private plane which seated six passengers.

Seeing how happy approaching the Jaguar, he asked if she would like to drive. You would have thought he said, "Hey you can have it." He handed her the keys and I can only imagine the smile on her face as she drove off with him beside her in the red two-seater Jaguar.

Upon returning to her car, she smiled and became sad all at once. When he asked what was wrong, she replied "Nothing." And yet she was sad to be leaving him.

She came home wondering if she would see him again. Would he call or did she just make him up? She kept saying out loud, "Who has that kind of money? Who looks that good and wasn't already married to some rich person?"

Just as she thought that out loud, she smiled to herself. God thank you for letting me be in the right place at the right time to meet Mr. Dillon Mason who has twelve cars and a plane.

Sky was a very private person and had only shared her dreams with Jasper and myself of one day owing that very car. She would say, "Once I finish school and secure a great paying job making at least six figures, I'm going to walk into a Jaguar dealership and say "I want that one please – yes the red one on the show room floor."

Whenever she spoke of wanting something, I would tell her to reach for the moon and you might get what you want. If you don't get the moon then a star or two will be just fine. But no matter which one you get, always be satisfied and thankful to the good LORD for allowing you to have it.

Every now and then I would remind her to always appreciate what GOD has given you and don't ever think about what others have as you don't know how they obtain it. Just be yourself and if it's meant to be, you'll get yours.

Sound to me like he was showing off - but I continue to listen. My instincts as a woman who worked all her life and as a mother warned me something was not right. Something bad was coming but ...I just didn't know what or when.

As Sky was telling me about her meeting and outing with Dillon – I was thinking, I guess she got the moon and the stars. Now I'm wondering if she was meant to have both at the same time.

I had a feeling that everything in the storage unit including the plane was leased to Mr. Mason. It was just a feeling but *oh* was the feeling strong.

Things Are Not Always What They

Appear To Be

CHAPTER TWO

IT WASN'T LONG after their meeting that Dillon had flowers and candy sent to her job every week. They dined at the most extravagant restaurants on a nightly basis. Never the same place twice within a span of three weeks. These were places Sky read about or saw on television but never dreamed she would be there one day.

After dinner they were always driven to various hotel lounges for coffee and dessert.

Six months had gone by, I became concerned, worried and suspicious. I had yet to meet this rich man that was dating my daughter and changing her little by little.

He took her shopping in Beverly Hills spending exorbitant amounts of money on her clothing, shoes and jewelry. It appears he never liked what she picked out or tried on and would encourage her to try something more to his liking, lifestyle and met with his approval.

As quickly as he said the words *I don't like*, clothes he had already chosen were in another dressing room waiting for her to try. And whether she liked them or not – that's what she ended up with and brought home.

Sky was young and taken in by all the excitement of being able to shop without looking at prices and she quickly became accustom to his lifestyle.

Red flag, bells and whistle were going off in my head as I listen to what they had done that day, as she showed me the clothes, shoes and accessories. Sky was happy so I kept quiet and let her be.

On one of her off days, Sky and I were at home in the kitchen having breakfast and discussing this new man in her life. I was happy that she was happy but always felt there was something about a man who has his own limo, chauffer, who could afford flowers arrangements that cost two to three hundred dollars and takes her shopping it seems like every day for something. Yes, I became very concern because Sky had not introduced me to Dillon.

"Why I had this strange feeling – I don't know but I did?"

At 8:30 that morning the doorbell rang. I ask Sky if she was expecting anyone. She shook her head no. I went to the door.

Upon opening the door there stood this beautiful woman, in a navy-blue suit. That suit had to cost fifteen hundred dollars if not more. She had on designer shoes, carried a designer purse and a few pieces of very expensive jewelry. She was absolutely stunning. I finally said, "Yes may I help you?"

In a very chipper voice she replied, "Hi I'm Catarina. I'm here to see Skylar Grant."

I called Sky.

Once Sky appeared, she introduced herself again and said, "Mr. Mason has paid for my services for the week to be your personal shopper."

"My what?" Again, this time a little louder she said **"My what and who sent you?"** Catarina repeated that Mr. Mason had paid for her services for the week to select a new wardrobe including evening gowns. She informed Sky that he was very specific about what he wanted and colors to be chosen.

Also, he has personally selected the hair stylist and makeup artist she was to use as of today and going forward and that their services had also been paid in advance. In that chipper voice she said, "As soon as you get dress we can leave and that she would be waiting in the limo."

The weekend was fast approaching and a messenger was sent to Sky job with a note from Dillon saying they would be attending a dinner dance in Bel Air.

A car would pick her, take her to the hair stylist, makeup artist, take her home to get dressed, then bring her to Bel Air where he would be waiting.

She was instructed to wear one of the gowns recently purchased along with the proper shoes and jewelry. Should she need help with accessorizing, contact Catarina and she would be there to assist.

So many things were going thru my mind and one thought stood out above the rest. Who has my child gotten involved with that can just tell you what to wear? To have your hair and makeup done at a moment notice. Was it because he purchases the clothes and all the other services? Who was Dillon Mason?

Dillon was creating his own Barbie doll. In my opinion this was not good. Not good at all.

————— ++++++ —————

Gossip and rumors were starting at her job and things were fast becoming bad for Sky. But she didn't care. She was happy.

Being in management for a number of years, I knew how rumors got out of hand, what it could do to your reputation. Eventually it would get all twisted and depending on your manger and the structure of management. It was only a matter of time before she would be dismissed for some reason or some kind of quick policy put together and approved by upper management. This would for sure be cause for immediate termination of employment.

I tried on several occasions to discuss my concerns about her taking so much time off, getting off work on short notice, being late and just not showing up.

Sky dismissed all my concerns.

She was happy, thought this was a dream when she met Dillon one hot day on Crenshaw Blvd.

He was constantly telling her there is more to come. Just be patient and I'll give you the world.

All the time I was thinking "
At what cost Sky? At what cost?"

*There Is Always A Motive
To What People Do When
It's Done For The Wrong Reason*

CHAPTER THREE

SKY KNEW I was anxious to meet Dillon. Without my knowing, she had arranged a meeting which would be taking place soon.

A few days later at 7:45 pm the doorbell rang. Standing there was a man I've never seen before dressed in a black suit, white shirt and tie. I looked down at his shoes and they were shinning like he just took them out of the box. Before he could speak, Sky came down and said, "Mommie I see you've met Gage." Gage is one of Dillon employees who is also his chauffeur.

Looking at Sky, she looked absolutely stunning in a beautiful evening gown of black satin with a matching shawl around her shoulders. Her neck was adorned with a single rope of diamonds and diamond studs in her ears that were just the right size to complement the ones around her neck.

Yes, she was a real-life size doll all dress up with a limo and chauffeur at her disposal.

As they were leaving, I noticed the neighbors had come outside on the porch and kids were in the street or sitting on the curb. Everyone it seems was staring at my house. I was thinking how nosy folks became when they see a limousine in our neighborhood, especially if no one has died. Or were they staring at Sky? Or both?

Gage opened the back door for Sky and once she was seated and the door closed, he walked around to get in the driver side. That's when I saw the two men on motorcycles in security uniforms in back of the limo.

As they were driving away, I was really starting to think who is Dillon Mason? This was a lot to take in as I watched them drive away and escorted.

My child was starting to look as though she belongs in Dillon Mason world. This was not Sky at all. What happen to the young lady who dressed in vintage clothing and hats and looked like she belonged on display? Where did she go?

One Saturday evening I notice huge garbage bags being brought down stairs and I wanted to know what was going on. Sky informed me that since Dillon had purchase her a new wardrobe, he insisted she give her other clothes to charity. Everything including her hats, gloves and shoes.

Then she added that I could have her old jewelry to use as I please since I was into crafts, redesign and sometimes added jewelry to clothes I made.

I wanted to know if that meant she was returning the pieces I and other family members had given her and she shook her head yes without looking at me. I silently took the box she handed me and walked away. That box of jewelry had sentimental value to her as it was handed down from generations. Unlike her giving everything away, this box was going to be kept. The more I thought about all this, the more I knew for sure – this was not good.

Since she was keeping erratic hours, I left a note on her bed and said, "I needed to meet Dillon so make it happen!" I remembered she had arranged for a meeting but it was not coming soon enough.

That feeling that something wasn't right continued to nag at me. I wanted to meet the man more than ever and could hardly wait until I did.

I found out a few days later that the event that was to be in Bel-Air was canceled and they flew to San Francisco instead for dinner. She had this smirk look on her face and I pray that smirk look was not intended for me.

Now imagine if you will the surprise look I had on my face and it was not a smirk.

CHAPTER FOUR

BECAUSE SKY WAS my only child, I might be over thinking this whole situation and needed to talk to someone that would try to help me make sense of what is going on.

So, I called Phoenix, my leveled headed sister. Up till now she had no knowledge of all what had taken place as I had given my word not to discuss this new found relation with anyone, especially Phoenix.

I finished my second cup of coffee, and I made the call. After the fifth ring she picked up and I looked toward the ceiling and mouth "Thank you."

I could tell immediately she was running late as usual, but took a few minutes to hear me out. Those few minutes turn in to thirty minutes then an hour.

I started telling Phoenix I could see little changes that probably no one else noticed. Then significant changes that actually started a few months into the relationship with Dillon. The hardest for me was when she stopped talking to me in the mornings. Now the most she would say was "I'll be back in a few days." No good morning. No good bye. No have a great day. No nothing."

I express my concern to Phoenix about the personal shopper, the limo, driver, the security escorts whenever they went out and about the drastic transfiguration of her wardrobe and style of dressing.

I told my sister it appears Dillon came from wealth or hit the lottery. He has the kind of money common folks only dream about _unless_ they won the lottery.

I wanted to know what was going on with Sky and this mystery man of hers. Was she getting caught up in his world of bright lights, glitz and glamor? I already knew the answer but had to ask the question out loud.

After I finish talking, I thought Phoenix had laid the phone down. When she finally spoke, all she said was "Wow!"

Wow is that all you have to say is wow?

Weren't you listening?

Should I repeat myself?

Sky is in a web of some sort. But right now, I really don't know what kind or what to think anymore. I don't want my baby to get hurt and wow is not an acceptable answer sister dear.

I need your advice as you're the level headed one that don't get upset and for sure don't let things bother you. You've been in school long enough to give sound advice so please say something other than **WOW!**

She laughed and with good reason. She was finishing her degree in Criminal Justice. Not Psychology. That was my field and yet here I am can't analyze or get my thoughts together.

After her laugher finally stop, she asks, "When did all this happen?"

Ok so she wasn't really listening as usual - only half hearing.

She too thought this was strange and would ask around if anyone knows Dillon Mason. She promises she would speak to her husband as he was in the entertainment industry and they both have close friends that often frequent places that Dillon has been taken Sky. Maybe some-one would know something.

After hanging up the phone a thought occurred to me. What hap-pen to Jasper? His name had not been brought up since Dillon.

Within two weeks, Phoenix reached out to me. No one in their immediate circle knew or even heard of Dillon Mason. She said, "Fie you are not going to like what I'm about to say." She was right I didn't. But I continue to listen as she was good with given advice when needed and sometimes when not warranted.

She told me I was too close to Sky to make a proper and true decision or opinion about Dillon. That I was afraid of losing her to an unknown person that no one knows anything about or have even heard of him. I should at least meet the man, get to know him before I make up my mind about his and Sky relationship. As for the drastic change with Sky, she surmised I was processing too much at one time.

Although the changed appears to happen overnight, it was in my mind. As we both know change occurs over time.

Before hanging up the phone, Phoenix said I have a lot of non-issue to work thru and she would help me any way she can. But for now, get a grip and wait it out to see where it goes. Be happy for your daughter.

I thought to myself - I can do that. Wait and see where it goes. But for how long should I wait before I say something? I'm already not liking the changes I see taken place.

Phoenix knew me all too well when it came to Sky. I didn't think clear and sometimes made rash and or harsh decisions. Maybe she was right. I raised her to be an independent person. A person to trust her own instinct and judgment. To examine all sides before making decisions.

But in my heart, I knew none of that happen. What I do know, she met a man like none of the young men around the neighborhood or in school. A man whose giving her everything she ever wanted. And like most people saw an opportunity and went for it.

After our conversation, I thought, maybe I am being too judgmental about the whole situation. Making quick decisions.

Each time I saw Sky smiling when she got dress to go out, I would think who wouldn't smile wearing designer clothing and accessories, a limo and driver at your disposal?

Oh well, the LORD will help me sort thru all this when it's time.

Be Anxious For Nothing

CHAPTER FIVE

ABOUT SIX MONTHS into the relationship, Sky came home one evening and ask me to come outside to see her new SUV. I said, "You're what? Girl you can't afford car payments on your salary." She just smiled and kept walking.

Outside was this beautiful black Lincoln Navigator with seats the color of caramel. It was indeed a beauty. I knew she couldn't afford something like this, let alone the upkeep. As if reading my mind, she said, "Mommie isn't it beautiful?" Dillon had it delivered to my job at lunchtime. My question was answered, without me asking.

She stood there just smiling and admiring her new SUV then said, "Let's go for a ride, then out to dinner and mommie wear one your new outfits I purchase for you."

Once again, talking to myself. This child is telling me what to wear as I climbed the stairs to go get changed.

When I looked thru my closet, I saw new clothes that were not my taste and Sky knew this. There were shoe boxes, bags with purses and on the corner of my dresser a new jewelry box, which I'm sure contain jewelry I didn't purchase. I would never have brought these things and had no intention of wearing any of it. Although truly beautiful but not my taste or style.

While getting dress in my own clothing, I felt there was more news to come, but I wasn't going to ask. I also knew I would have to restrain and prepare myself to sit and listen.

When I came downstairs, I noticed Sky had on a new outfit. When she saw me, she said, "Mommie you are not wearing that are you? I want to take you to a nice dinner." I told her what I had on was just fine and I was not changing.

As we drove out of the neighborhood, I notice we were going near the water. Then I saw a sign that read Malibu.

This was interesting. I see why Sky wanted me to put on a new outfit. These people were elegantly dress and personally I thought over dress to be near the water eating at a seafood restaurant.

Once inside I felt as though everyone was looking at me and I'm sure they were, compared to the way Sky was dressed I looked like the hired help and yet I held my head up as we were escorted to the patio area.

There Is Greatness In Not Caring

What People Think

I Was Always Told To Be
Proud Of Who I Am

Never Hold Your Head
Down For Anyone

In Any Situation!

And just for a few seconds I wanted to run and hide.
There was that feeling again.

———— ·+++++·· ————

All thru dinner I was anxiously waiting for Sky to tell me what was going on. When coffee was served Sky informed me she had been fired for some time from her job and was going to work with Dillon. Not sure I heard her correctly I asked her to repeat the last part. She said, "I'm going to work with Dillon."

So, my hearing was not gone. She did say **with** him not for him. I asked, "Exactly what does that mean working with him?"

I asked her about school? She informed me Dillon would make sure she stays in school. At that I laugh. I asked her if she heard herself talking or did, she memorizes all this?"

None of the answer given made sense to me.

This child had made up her mind and at that moment I was in no mood to argue. I got up from the table and said I would be waiting outside for her to take me home.

She tried talking to me on the way home and I ask her to stop talking.

The ride home was very quiet and strained. I was very uncomfortable riding with Sky for fear I might say something I would regret later. This was the first time I can remember becoming this irate with her and at this time I didn't like being around my own child. It was if I know longer knew who she was or had become.

Anger Locks You Into A World

Where You Can No Longer Speak

Finally

The Day Arrives When I

Would Meet The Man Himself Who

Changed

Skylar Grant

CHAPTER SIX

SEVERAL MONTHS HAD gone by before Sky announced Dillon was coming to Thanksgiving dinner. It should be ready around four as they have plans for later that day. She asked me to be nice. Made a few suggestions of what I should wear too dinner. Now that hit a nerve.

After cooking the previous night and finishing up today she requested I dress up! Somewhere in time she has lost her mind. Telling me to be nice. What I should wear in my own house, never mind telling me what time dinner should be ready. Yep. Lost her mind or fell and bumped her head. **HARD!**

Standing speechless since we had not talked to each other since the dinner in Malibu, I could have screamed with her demands. *Thinking to myself - oh my dear Sky that is not going to happen.* But it was nice of you to think it's going to happen.

At last I finished cooking dinner which consisted of baked ham, baked hen and dressing, cranberry sauce, turnips and mustards, candied yams, whiskey rolls, potato salad, ice tea, and sweet potato pies.

I asked her to set the dining room table with an extra place setting. Too my amazement she did without a word. And I was thankful others would be present when the man himself arrived. As for me, I was more than ready to meet him.

As **I** was getting dress, I found myself starting to get nervous as I had no idea what to expect. What I didn't want that day was a limo parked out front with security.

At precisely 4 pm the doorbell rang and Sky rushed downstairs to answer the door. She had changed clothes and was dress in a beautiful outfit of blue. I found out later it was tailor made by his tailor just for Sky.

In the foyer stood this gorgeous man of 6' 3 with the most beautiful head of wavy hair. Not a strand out of place. Beautiful smile and snow-white teeth – the whitest I had ever seen. His navy suit was of very fine material. Not the kind you see in men shops. There was something different about it. His blue and white plaid shirt had a starch white collar with 4-inch white cuffs held together with cuff links with initials, **DM.**

Upon further inspection, the cuff links held a single blue stone surrounded by diamonds. His shoes the same color as his suit. I noticed the rings on his hands, looked up at him, and for the first time noticed he was my age!

WHAT THE HELL!!!!

This man of mystery is my age. I could tell my looking at his hands. You can disguise your entire body with a makeover ALL but the hands and feet. At least not yet anyway.

I see why Sky was so taken with his good looks. He very mature and with maturity comes your natural looks. You rarely see men my age that has taking care of themselves to this level.

But wait a minute…he was not from our part of town. He's from Beverly Hills. You see on tv commercials of men having plastic surgery more so than women. I begin to wonder if he was one of those men.

I stood there staring at him until I heard Sky say, "Mommie this is Dillon, Dillon this is my mom Fiona." I held out my hand to him and he did something that caught me off guard. He pulls me to him in a warm embrace and said, "It's nice to finally meet the mother of the woman I love." Upon releasing me, he placed a small box in my hand. I was speechless but not impressed as says, "A gift for our mother."

When I was finally out of his embrace, I stepped back and looked from Sky to him then back at Sky hoping she was able to tell from my posture or expression on my face I was not pleased and was appalled by the verbiage mother of the woman he loved. One more time I looked at him then at Sky. I said nothing to either of them about that remark… at least for now. I had no expression on my face that I'm sure was pleasing. Just a blank stare. No nod, shaking of my head or a smile. Just a blank stare at both of them.

When I looked at Sky, I noticed she was dressed in the color that compliments what he was wearing as she put on her diamond studs and laid her clutch on the hall table. I knew without a doubt that was his idea that they should wear colors that complement him.

He was everything Sky had describe him to be down to his smile, except for one thing, he was my age!

I took a quick look outside and to my surprise he was alone. No limo. No security. Instead I saw a car I didn't recognize. Midnight blue and beautiful. I learned later from my friend it was a Maserati.

I had a lot of resentment toward this man but knew the time to voice my opinion was not now. Today was a day of discovery. A chance to find out who this man was that had the power to change my child. Or did she willing go because of his charm and money?

I had forgotten I was holding the gift he had given me and laid it on the kitchen counter.

Once Sky saw the gift, she asked me to open it. I said, "After dinner." Of course, she asked me a few more times and I gave her the look that meant stop talking. Finally, there was silence from her as I put the box in the drawer. (Which I forgot it was there...oops).

As Sky escorted him into the living room to meet the family and my friend, Marvin, I was left with three thoughts:

1. He is too old for Sky.

2. Who in the world has teeth that white and straight?

3. Who dresses for Thanksgiving dinner in a suit and diamond cuff links?

Dillon definitely was not shy. He acted as though his mere presence demanded attention and that's just what he got from my family. He was a talker with a hearty laugh. His was the only voice and laughter I heard coming from the living room.

At 5:15 we all headed to the dining room, he complemented our home. He said it reminded him of his nanny house as it was very similar to this one. He kept complementing me on the food. Again, his nanny was brought into the conversation by saying she cooked food like this all time. He believed it was called soul food and found it delicious. I noticed he was careful not to mention the nanny name but said several times she raised him.

My mind was racing and in over drive. Now was the perfect time to ask questions. But because family and guest were present, I thought it best to wait.

Prayer was usually said my dad before dinner but Dillon insisted upon blessing the food. When he opened his mouth the words that came out were surreal. Whatever I had been thinking about him vanish. I was taken in by Dillon and yet I question myself why? What happen during that pray?

Once the prayer was over, Sky fixed his plate and he told her how much food was to go on there and exactly where to put it. She looked like she was trained for this. I looked in amazement as everyone else did, especially since the food was placed on the table and to be served buffet style.

As Dillon finishes his first serving of food, without him saying a word I noticed Sky get up and refilled his plate. If his water or tea glass was empty, he would point and it was immediately refilled by her. No one said anything but my sister and I looked at each other in awe.

All thru dinner he was the prefect dinner guest. He talked about his life with his nanny but never mentioned his parents. He told us he grew up in Beverly Hills, travels abroad regularly, that he personally owns several businesses but fail to mention names or locations also that he owns a few rental houses in the surrounding area but being careful not to mention the city.

When he talked about his schooling, I knew for certain he was my age. If not, he was so close that he'll break the numbers apart.

I looked over at Sky, then around the table and all eyes were on Dillon Mason. Everyone was nodding their head except Phoenix. She caught me staring at him and we both shook our heads. Even my dad was quiet and listening and he doesn't like to sit for long anywhere.

Dillon kept saying I haven't had this type of food since I was a child living with my nanny. He kept complementing the food until I actually stop listening. Last thing I heard him ask if I cooked or was it catered?

Upon hearing that statement, I looked at him and said, "Yes Dillon I cooked the entire dinner. We don't have food catered in for the holidays." Sky saw the look on my face and quickly replied, "My mom is an excellent cook, she doesn't like too but when she does – she's excellent."

Why in the world does she have to explain anything to him about me?

Before dessert and coffee was served, everyone was leaving as they had other places to stop. I ask Marvin to leave as I wanted to speak with Dillon and Sky in private.

I never spoke to Marvin about Sky or Dillon as we were just starting to get to know one another. And from what I've seen so far from him and the question he asked, Marvin would rather stay and be part of the conversation and I was not ready for that or need more to think about as this was just between the three of us.

Once everyone had left, I clean the table and put out dessert and coffee. Sky fixed Dillon a dessert plate but no coffee all the while explaining Dillon only drinks coffee from certain coffee houses after his dinner. That clears up the mystery of why she didn't pour him a cup.

He made a point to tell me he eats breakfast, lunch and dinner out every day at various four- or five-star restaurants. He doesn't eat or like fast food. Not even snacks.

Where he ate and the star of the restaurants didn't interest me and I believe he knew it. I was not impressed with his status only about Sky.

Since he wanted me to know certain things, I wanted to know what he wasn't saying.

So, I asked Dillon to tell me about himself, his family and how he came to be in the Crenshaw area?

Instead of answering my questions he wanted to know if he could call me mother as he felt like part of the family already and how much he loved Sky.

In a calm voice I replied, "Dillon you may address me as Fiona or Ms. Grant but not mother." If looks could kill Sky probably would have put me in an early grave. However, she knew not to say a word, correct me or even look at me.

With my questions unanswered, he grinned at me, stood up, hug me and thank me for a wonderful evening and then he **deliberated** called me "Mother". Sky looked at me and smiled. I looked at her and I'm sure I had some type of expression on my face but it was not a smile. Just like that they both left.

When she returned several hours later, I was waiting to talk with her. I felt I've been quiet too long and as her mom I had to say my peace. I knew it would lead to a knock down drag out on my part as Sky had turn a deaf ear whenever I brought up his name.

As she walked pass me and didn't speak, I demanded that she come sit down, listen and not talk till I'm finish. Before I could say anything, she started defending Dillon. I guess she didn't her me tell her not to talk till l finish.

Because she ignored me, the pent-up anger came front and center and once again I informed her that I would appreciate if she would not interrupt me while I'm talking and not to run out of the room.

Now that I had her attention, I told her my first concern was the twenty plus age difference. This man has lived a full and productive life compared to your twenty-two years.

Sky just sat there staring into space not looking at me. I told her I was concern about his finances as it was obvious, he doesn't have a nine to five job. Since you are now working "**With**" him what exactly are you doing? Where does he get his money? How does he get his money? Are you still in school?

Sky looked at me with hatred in her eyes. With a voice in nasty undertones she said, "That is none of your business mother." She slowly rose out of the chair and said, "Are you thru talking to me? I have to get pack as I'm leaving for a few days with Dillon on a business trip."

I replied, "No, I am not. Please sit down. This is my house and I'm still your mom. Not your "mother", so please sit back down. The packing can wait.

I continued with there was something wrong about a man having that kind of wealth and can't or want say how it came to be. When I asked him about his family, he completely ignored the question with a laugh and smile. I can't recall what he said to you, but I remember clearly the look you gave me. One of those how could you looks. I'm sure it embarrassed you and for that I'm **not** sorry. I know you are grown but you need to wake up."

There was so much more I wanted to say but stopped. I informed her I was done talking for now and that she may leave the room.

Before leaving she said, "Mother in the future you may speak to me in a tone much nicer. If you feel you cannot comply with my request or not pleased with what I'm doing – do not speak to me at all." She knew I hated the word ***mother*** and she did it on purpose. She also knew me enough to go up the stairs and close the door quickly before I got out of my chair.

I sat there fuming and slowly breathing as I didn't want to become nervous or anxious from dealing with her behavior especially over a man. I was still trying to figure out when that girl was going to come to her senses and realize the world and environment, she is living right may be good. But what about her future. I wanted her to be careful.

I learned over the years if something comes to you easy – you don't appreciate it until it's gone. And my instinct as a woman and mom is telling me Mr. Mason had or has everything handed to him and has earn none of it.

Sky was slowly letting go of everyone she knew from her past including Jasper, who she had been dating for four years.

I wanted to scream but decided against it. Time was on my side. I know that in order to get thru this …whatever "this" is, prayer was needed and a lot of it. I didn't like who she had become and I was not going to accept it. I didn't care for him but he was dating my daughter so I too had to be careful and chose my words carefully.

Yes, I had a lot of questions about that man, his companies, family and now Skylar Grant. What exactly did he do for a living? What exactly was Sky doing for a living?

After she left, I needed some me time. I needed to think about the day's event. I took a hot shower. Tired to watch television to relax and it didn't work.

I sat in the dark and practice deep breathing as I was really uptight, talking out loud, and asking questions that may or may not get answered.

The rest of the night all I could think about was this older man, my age, saying he's in love with a woman twenty plus years younger and how he transformed her into a trophy of his own design.

Thinking back, I was really hung up on the age difference because I've seen what can happen when you become someone's trophy. Jealousy and mistrust always play a part before destruction occurs.

As for the trophy – it's my child.

Emotions Last Ninety Seconds Or So

They Say...

But It Ain't So

Yes, I said it ain't so

CHAPTER SEVEN

I WOULD LOOK into Sky room hoping she would be there but on so many nights she never made it home.

This made me angry and yet she was an adult and no longer a child. But the mom in me said, maybe, but you're still my baby girl.

One day I looked in her room, I noticed a garment bag laying on the bed and a shopping bag on the floor.

I open the garment and saw a beautiful a chiffon gown with diamonds and pearls sewed into the neckline forming a V. At the bottom of the bag was a black velvet pouch with a strand of pearls and matching earrings. In the shopping bag were shoes and a purse.

The price tags were still attached so I did the math. Total cost of items made me take a seat near the window as I needed to look out at street and see if I was asleep or really looking at bodacious prices. I was not dreaming or imaging any of this. All these items cost more than I made in a year.

OK BREATH FIONA

BREATH 1 2 3

BREATH 1 2 3

DON'T GIVE IN TO THOSE EMOTION

BREATH 1 2 3

DON'T THINK JUST BREATH

1 2 3

Chapter Eight

THE NEXT FEW weeks I was in total awe still thinking of the hefty price tags on a few items.

I had a lot on my mind and discovered that thinking about Dillon took up a lot of my time. I had given my previous three question a hard pass and now I wanted to know: **1**) Who are you Dillon Mason and **2**) What's your end game?

Still thinking about the situation, I realize Dillon could have any woman he wanted. And yet he chose to come downtown. What's wrong with the women of power and stature from uptown where he resides?

Immediately I felt bad and angry with myself for even thinking that way. Sky appeared to be happy. She was getting everything she wanted and more. I should be happy for her but it didn't seem right. Something felt wrong.

Sky was still living at home but slowly becoming a stranger. I couldn't talk to her without one of us getting angry and of course she would escape to her room, pack a bag and leave. Each time this happen days turned into weeks before her return home.

I knew it would be a matter of time before Sky moved out. She hardly ever spoke when she came in or was leaving. No note – just the sound of the door closing. I had become accustom to the silent treatment.

All my questions went unanswered; therefore, I have to take a different approach with her when asking questions if I want a direct answer.

The Sky I knew was gone. Her signature look gone and replace by Dillon who insisted she wear more conservative colors and clothing, exquisite jewelry and evening gowns of his choice depending on the event. Hair and makeup done every day. Nails and feet done weekly so the polish match her clothes.

After weeks had gone by, I ask Sky if she was comfortable with the change in her appearance. She stared, smiled and said, "You wouldn't understand mother so I want bother to explain." But she never answered my question.

I thought to myself, *oh Sky you don't understand.* You don't see all that has taken place. You only see what Dillon has allowed you to see. So, my little one - you are WRONG. Now it was my turn to stare at her and smile. Then I walked away from her. Something she wasn't use too.

A month later, Dillon had his secretary call to invite Marvin and myself to dinner that week. The day would be my choice. I replied, "I would check my calendar and get back with you shortly."

I immediately called Phoenix and told her what just happen and asked what night she was free as she was going to be my quest for the evening instead of Marvin.

I returned the call, informed whomever answered the phone, my sister and I would be free for dinner this Thursday. She replied, a car would pick us up at seven and dinner would be at eight. Before I could ask where dinner was going to be – she hung up.

CHAPTER NINE

SOME TIME AGO I had a dream about Dillon. In my dream he was the devil, laughing at me, pointed his finger and said. "Soon." Now what the hell did that mean?

As she still had her room, Sky came home the week of the scheduled dinner with two garment bags and two large shopping bags.

Before going upstairs as she done so many times without speaking, she actually spoke and said, "Hello mom," and I almost fell out my chair. I was in a state of shock that it took me a few minutes to compose myself before saying anything. I didn't want a lot of questions flying out my mouth. I was still angry with her and didn't want to spoil this dinner or fight with her before I had a chance to meet Dillon again and hear what he had to say, if anything.

I watched as she went up the stairs. I could hear her opening and closing the doors. This went on for about thirty minutes before she came back down stairs where I was sitting drinking coffee.

My heart was beating with joy as she sat down opposite me until she opens her mouth and said, "I brought you a gown to wear to dinner tomorrow night." My heart sank. I swallowed hard and said, "Thank you."

I really wanted to say what's wrong with the clothes or gowns I have? It's just dinner. But thought against it as I didn't want to be ignored and have her go into silent mode.

Later that evening, I went upstairs to see what had been chosen for me to wear. Hanging on the closet door was the most beautiful evening gown I had seen as I definitely owned nothing like this.

It was a red satin gown with a V cut in back with what appeared to be hand sewn rhinestones outlining the V. (it appears "they" like the

V cut). Behind the gown was a red and white satin shawl with pockets. On the floor were shoes. On the bed was the purse with a note on top. The note read – look inside. There was a gold chain necklace with a solitaire diamond and matching earrings. I was speechless and almost forgot to breath.

I had to call Phoenix and let her know the dinner was definitely going to be formal.

I didn't know Sky had been standing in the doorway until she said, "I'm glad you like everything.

By now I'm sure you know or have guest all Dillon clothes are custom made and so are a few of my gowns. While he was having a suit made for dinner, he wanted you to have something special to wear as well so he called and ordered you this gown from his favorite store."

Instead of thank you coming out of my mouth, I just shook my head. Once I heard his name the dress was no longer beautiful and certainly held no sentimental value to me regardless of what outlandish price everything cost.

She knew how I felt about Dillon. But she was home and I didn't want to argue about a gown. I was just glad she was home even if for a little while. I was very glad to look at her.

Later that evening I was starting to wonder what type of dinner am I attending and why? I kept having bad feelings that something wasn't right. That one day the devil would show his true form in the body of Dillon Mason.

———— ◆◆◆◆ ————

I was about to call Phoenix when the phone rang and a voice said, "Ms. Grant you have a two pm hair and nail appointment with Ms Grant hair stylist and manicurist." She gave me the address and requested I not be late. I was thinking – what no car to pick me up??

Now who wanted this done him or her?

CHAPTER TEN

DID HE HAVE everyone on his payroll?

Didn't Sky know I still had a regular job and taking off for a hair appointment was not in or on my to do list?

Then I laugh to myself and thought oh LORD here I go again talking out loud to myself. One of these days those two will have me laying on a shrink couch if I don't watch myself.

Suddenly I remembered I hadn't called my sister.

I phoned Phoenix and describe my outfit in details and was hoping she could picture everything as I was describing too her. I told her to dress for the evening. To wear the gown, she purchases on her last shopping trip to New York.

At last it was Thursday. As I stared in the mirror at myself, I must admit I looked pretty good for a lady my age. I wished my James was alive to see me. I said into the mirror, "James if you can hear me, be with me tonight and keep me safe. When you hear me talking too much wrap your arms around me so I can feel your presence and know it's time to sit still and be quiet".

The doorbell rang at precisely seven pm.

There stood Gage.

He held out his hand as I walked down the steps. I immediately looked right and left to see if my neighbors were looking and yes, they were all outside. I straighten up and walked with my head up as I know for once in my life, Fiona Grant was looking fabulous.

Gage escorted me to a white limo and held the back door open for me. Once Gage had gotten in the driver seat, he informed me he was going to pick up Mrs. Phoenix Anderson.

As soon the limo turned the corner, I called Phoenix and said, "You're not going to believe this so I want spoil the surprise. We're on our way to your house."

Now I've been in limos before but only the ones taken from the airport to my various job assignments when working out of town. But those limos don't even come close to this one.

I could have lived in this limo for a few days and never miss my bed.

So, this is what Sky was getting accustom too. I just smiled and put my head back.

I heard a faint noise and noticed Gage had put on soft jazz. The music was coming thru very nicely. He let down the partition to inform me Mr. Mason had stocked the bar with champagne, wine, fruit and cheese for us to enjoy on the way to dinner. The lights were turned off overhead and soft white lights surrounded the entire back of the limo. That's when I noticed the carpet was red which made the white leather seats stand out.

When the car turned the corner, I looked out the smoked windows and saw we were approaching Phoenix house. And just like my street, a few folks walking had stopped to watch as the white limo stopped in front of my sister house.

I couldn't wait to see the expression on Phoenix face and she didn't disappoint. Her face had this ginormous grin. I don't know if it was for the limo, the fact that Gage was holding out his well-manicured hand for her or his good looks and accent.

She climbed into the limo looking very chic in her black dress and hair pinned up. After she finally stopped grinning, she looked around the limo in awe. I offered her a glass of champagne or wine, fresh fruit and cheese from the bar. We both laugh. Both thinking the same thing. Where are we going for dinner?

Forty minutes later we arrived at our destination and the back door open.

Once out of the limo we were staring at the most beautiful magnificent hotel and restaurant we had ever seen. It was truly amazing. The sheer scenery itself was breath taking and as we began to walk to the front entrance, we heard the waves of the ocean.

As we reached the door, the doorman opens the door and it was if we stepped back in time. The foyer was exquisite. While standing in the foyer we were approached by a gentleman that informed us Mr. Mason and guest was waiting in the dining area. We followed him and of course looking and taking in everything we saw. I was most amused by the paintings on the wall. Soon we were in the largest and most breathe taking dining room with a stage which held an orchestra.

I saw Sky coming toward us and as I reached out to embrace her, in three strides Dillon was there and hugged both Phoenix and myself. I saw Sky step back and said how delighted she was to see us. Not glad but delighted. My smile turns quickly to a smirk as I wanted a hug from Sky not HIM.

To make matters worse with laughter in her voice she whispers, "Mother I'm so glad you and auntie are here. Dillon just ordered drinks. You looked beautiful mother and I'm glad you wore the gown. Dillon said he knew that color would look stunning on you and he picked out the accessories. Don't you just love it?" (This is the second time she mentions Dillon and the gown) Right then and there I wanted to pull off the dress and all that went with it.

Damn that man! I just smiled. I never said a word.

I didn't think or let my emotion gets the better of me that night. I decided to relax, watch, listen and enjoy the evening. I've noticed it before that Sky on occasion had start calling me mother. I dislike that word more and more.

Dillon order a bottle of Dom for the table and when it arrive the mai*tre d poured. There were no menus handed out as he had taken the liberty to order for everyone.

Phoenix whispered to me, "What if I don't like what he ordered? I would like to see a menu please?"

The mai*tre d looked at Dillon and he nodded yes. She didn't order but read everything on the menu. I know her pretty well. She was looking at the prices.

Sky looked over at Phoenix then at me and starting telling us there was really no need to order as Dillon has selected a wonderful dinner selection, desert and wine to compliment the dinner. And then directly to me - mother he knows you don't care for seafood and he ordered you something different. I know you both will enjoy the dinner he has chosen.

Ok Sky how long have you been discussing me with 'him" and how much have you told him?

Food started arriving and they were right, we both enjoyed everything, even the desert. This was the best tasting food I've eaten in a long time.

Afterward he ordered me coffee while the three of them continue to drink wine.

I'm sure it was a mistake that the wine menu was left on the table, so I took a peek. The wine they were drinking cost five hundred and fifty dollars a bottle and they were on the second one. I guess that's why my sister was enjoying it so much.

Phoenix and I excused ourselves to go to the ladies' room. I ask Sky if she would join us and without taking her eyes off Dillon replied no.

After four hours of being entertain it was time for us to leave. We all walked out together and I was excited we would all be riding back together. Then to my surprise only Phoenix and I got in the limo. Dillon leaned in and said, " We're staying over for a few days as I have business to attend in the area."

Sky said, "Mother you really do look divine tonight and handed me an envelope and whispered, "Take care, we love you."

As if on cue Gage drove off.

I looked at Phoenix and she could see I didn't want to talk as I lean my head back and closed my eyes. There were hot tears slowly coming down as I held the envelope in my hand. I could hear jazz music softly playing in the back ground. Phoenix called her husband and was telling him about our evening. Finally, I took out a bottle of unopen wine and poured me a large glass.

When we arrived at Phoenix, Gage open the door for her and waited until she was inside before driving away in the direction of my home. Once we arrive, he escorted me to my door, waited till I open the front door, said good night, turned and walked away.

I realize I still had the envelope in my hand unopen as I entered my bedroom. Sky had written on the envelope – We love you Mother. I looked at it for a while and placed it in my night stand along with the others I had been given over a period of time. I was thinking "I "was now "we" and now I'm mother instead of mom or mommie.

At that moment I realize things will never be same. I have to accept and move on. In my heart I knew Sky was now living in Dillon world. Whatever world that may be. But definitely not the one she was brought up in.

You Can't Focus On The Pass.

You Can't Go Back And Fix It.

What's Done Is Done!

CHAPTER ELEVEN

I HAD TO get my life back on track and find normalcy and equilibrium. Right now, I had to focus on myself or go crazy worrying about Sky and what was taking place in her life.

Whatever it was, I know she was not about to tell me fore she knew I wouldn't approve. So, it's in my best interest to keep busy and find the norm that would allow me some inter peace.

A few weeks later, she returned home for a visit. Her hair had been cut with at least twelve inches taken off and styled. Although it looked beautiful, I was shocked as she had never cut her hair only had it trimmed. She saw the expression on my face and quickly said, "Dillon wanted me to have my hair cut and style to complement my new wardrobe." He assured her the new look would show off her features and make up better.

That night they were going to see a play. After the play she, meaning they, would like for me to join them for dinner afterwards. She would phone of the time and a car would be picking me up.

Now when did this happen that I was no longer given a choice if I wanted to go or not? It sounded like a demand rather than a request. But I went along with it. Now sometimes I wonder why. Maybe to be near Sky.

This sadden me greatly that a man can have that kind of control over another person. I don't think she realize how caught up she was in "his" world. Whenever she speaks now its Dillon this or Dillon that and **mother**.

While waiting for her to come downstairs I was remembering when we would sit and talk for hours, going to the mall, long walks, flea markets or the movies. On Fridays she would be planning her weekend with the girls or going out with Jasper.

Now when she comes over there are always garment bags and several shopping bags. As she was going up the stairs, she stopped to inform me a box was placed on my bed and I was to wear it to dinner. This girl had gotten on my nerves always telling me what to wear as if I didn't know how to dress.

As I climbed the stairs, anger slowly built up inside and I thought it best not to speak. I didn't want to become conformational as I'm sure I would regret it later. Besides, I wanted to see where all this was leading.

My intuition as a mom never changed or wavered about him and my concerns for Sky well-being continue to grow. My thoughts were always the same. I was slowly being convince that Dillon was the devil or at least one of the top-ranking officers.

Sky followed me into my room said, "Mother I brought this because I wanted you to look nice to night. We're taking you to the Marina to eat at our favorite spots." Which translate to his favorite restaurant.

I told her I would go if she promises to stop calling me mother. She looked at me and said, "It's just a term of endearment." I'm not sure if she heard me **but** I heard her. I repeated myself this time with authority in my voice, *"I will go if you stop calling me mother."*

We stared at each other for what seems like hours but it was only a few seconds as she knows "mother" has had enough of being called "mother". Sky knew how far to push me and gave in reluctantly or so I thought. She left my bedroom and close the door.

Not only did I dislike Dillon Mason but I'm starting to resent everything about my child especially her clothes. (Sounds like I'm jealous...no momma is furious)

————————— ‧✦✦✦‧ —————————

Sky called after the play. I showered and changed into the clothes she or he had purchased. Looked into the mirror and thought this is not Fiona Grant. The outfit was stunning but not for me. Not my colors or style. This was Dillon choice as I've seen Sky in these colors lots of time. Black and cream. Sky knows my style in dressing but I surmise this was all Dillon.

I truly disliked this man until my insides were on fire. I didn't know how much longer I would be able to deal with any of this.

I turn my mind from Dillon and started thinking about Sky. I wanted to know how she was spending her days. What was she doing working with Dillon? I know school was no longer a part of her life. Although Dillon had told her she would continue going to school. That turned out to be a lie.

Dillon had changed everything about Sky. Her hair, vintage clothing even the car she had brought herself – all gone.

Her wardrobe now consists of only black, navy, cream, brown. All dresses or skirts. No slacks or jeans. She was too young to wear those colors every day and not own a pair of slacks, jeans not even a pair of shorts. *I was too young to wear those colors every day.*

Everything she wore was hi-end or tailored made. Even her shirts and jackets. I notice one day her shirts had her initials on the cuff and she now wore cuff links. He had given her a black card of her very own and was paying the bill. Up till now I had never heard of a black card.

Thinking back - two years ago Sky dress in vibrant and happy colors. She was like my fashion consultant when I went shopping. Those days are gone. On those rare occasion when I see Sky, her style of dressing is very professional. On special occasions which was about seventy percent of the time they both had on the same or coordinating colors. He was always smiling but my Sky was not. She looks sad.

I should have been happy that she was sad but as a mom, I know there was reason and only time would tell why.

I started thinking I could have been a better mom or maybe I should have done this or that and just maybe this wouldn't be taking place. Those were my feelings and I shared them with no one not even my closest friend La 'niece. I started experiencing empty feelings of loneliness because Sky was never home.

I called Phoenix and we talked into the night like we used to when we were teenagers. Only this time it was me talking and she listen quietly.

After about thirty minutes I asked if she was still there. She replied, "Yes Fie I'm still here.' I'm thinking about all we've talked about, what we've done with those two and how much Sky has changed. You know this is not good. I got a bad feeling it's not going to end well and you sister should be careful."

We said our good nights and I thought about her warning to be careful. Be careful of what and of whom? Sky or Dillon? Little did I know the warning and of whom was wrong. I should have been careful of them both.

To keep from being lonely and against my better judgement, I asked Marvin would he like to move in with me and give up his apartment. Within the month he was there.

A BIG MISTAKE ON MY PART but loneliness makes you do irrational things.

Find a place where there's joy

and the joy will burn

out the pain

CHAPTER TWELVE

A FEW MONTHS later Sky had gone to the house to get some of her personal things and notice Marvin car parked out front. Another car in the drive way. She had her key so she walked in. What she witnessed was Marvin and a woman in the den making out like teenagers. Both completely naked and so busy neither notice her standing there.

She said after she got their attention, she called me to tell what she had just witness.

I was in total shock and that was putting it mildly. I immediately left my office headed home.

An hour or more had passed and I was still sitting in my car in the garbage of my office building. I could see people walking and talking, going in and out of the building but I couldn't move. My body had gone into shock and yet I felt betrayed and mad as hell.

My cell phone rang. It was Sky inquiring if I had left. I informed her I was in my car in the parking structure but didn't want to drive just yet. She knew I had assigned parking and where I would be and said they would come get me.

Twenty minutes later I heard a knock on my window and unlock the door. For the first time in three years my daughter actually hugged me and said how sorry she was as we walked to her SUV.

As we approach the house Sky said in a calm voice, "Mom it's going to be ok." Then another voice said, "We're getting you out of that house mother." Only then did I notice Dillon sitting in the back seat. He was smiling with black sunglasses on and looking straight ahead.

When I got home, no one was there. I phoned Phoenix, explained what happen and within the hour she was there. She put her arms around me and only then did I cry.

It seems I was crying about everything that had taken place. What just happen in my house just made matters worse. It seems like my life was falling apart and I was going with it. I believe everything happens for a reason. But for now, it was too much to process.

I blamed Marvin for his stupidity. Without questions or answers from him it was over. There was no coming back from this. We were over. Done.

I wanted to blame Dillon for his part in destroying my life. Maybe for all of it. He had come into my perfect uncomplicated life and slowly started taking it apart.

It all started that day when he met a beautiful young woman name Skylar Grant on a street corner. But I knew what Marvin had done was not Dillon fault.

I discuss the idea of moving with Phoenix to get a new start. Then spoke to Sky that I would be looking for a place to move, putting the house up for rent until I decided what I wanted to do.

She squealed with delight at the thought of me moving and wanted us to find a place in Beverly Hills. Without realizing my voice was raised, "Girl have you lost your mind. Beverly Hills on my salary?" She assured me between the two us splitting the rent we could do this.

But Beverly Hills Sky really? I thought you moved in with Dillon and had a place to stay now your saying us.

I was thinking back to the time I saw how sad she looked. Maybe things were not going well or she sees what I've been seeing. Her slowly becoming someone else.

*Consider it pure joy, my
brothers and sisters.*

*Whenever you face trails
of many kinds,*

*Because you know that
the testing of your*

Faith produces preservice

James 1:2-3 KJV

With EVERYTHING that's going on – I truly believe my faith was
being tested.

After thinking about it for a few days I told Sky to go ahead and see what's affordable. Within two weeks Sky had found a place in Beverly Hills with zip code 90211.

I agreed to go see the place and to my surprise it was a beautiful townhouse. It had two master bedrooms, a guest room, extra bathroom and two separate balconies. I loved it. Before the smile became permanent on my face, I asked the rental cost followed immediately by have you lost your mind?

This had to be a joke or a hidden camera somewhere. I could not afford a place like this on my salary. But if I could this would be it. I remembered she would be paying half but with the way things have been going and she's not their eighty percent of the time – I really couldn't afford to take chances.

Sky assured me not to worry about the money as it was all taken care of as she and Dillon had discussed it already. And yet the leasing agreement was in my name. She reminded me again she would be helping pay rent and expenses. I was waiting for the punch line and it came a quicker than I had anticipated. Before the big move the "I" turned into "us'. And the **us** meant Dillon.

She explained he would be staying there for a day or two every other week as he owned several properties in the surrounding area.

He would pay her half and I of course would pay the other. I was thinking why he can't pay the entire thing? Just as quickly as that thought came in my head, I dismissed it because I didn't want to owe him anything as my feelings toward him had not changed. However, living in the same place would give me a better opportunity to know Dillon Mason.

Within three weeks I had a Beverly Hills address with underground parking, swimming pool, hot tub and masseur on the premise. I took two weeks off work and Sky was there every day to help set up house and unpack. True to her word Dillon was there for a day or two every other week.

Our new home was more breathtaking each time I entered. I couldn't wait for Phoenix to come over and enjoy the view and amenities. I was constantly having an awe moment and when Phoenix came over to see the place, she was very pleased.

One day while driving to work it occurred to me that I might actually learn to like the man since I don't have to be in his immediate surrounding every day. This would allow me the opportunity to give him a fair chance. I know my dislike for him helped push Sky straight to him.

And just as quickly as those thoughts occurred, they went away. I was not going to blame myself for everything that has taken place. I was a good mom and I knew it. I gave her what I could afford and taught her the difference between want and need.

Dillon came along and gave her both. Wants and needs. I didn't cry often but this time there were tears. I made a promise that I would try to get along with Dillon. I truly felt if I didn't, he would destroy my family even more.

Later that day I phone Sky and said, "I wanted to cook something special for the two of them and expected dinner to be at seven." She phoned back that Dillon had made reservations for us at eight thirty that same night.

So much for my plans. It seems that he has overridden my request. Silent I was fuming inside and shook my head as I replace the phone on the receiver.

I had made a promise to try and get along with "him" and I was determined to do my best.

To keep my word for as long as I could. This was going to be a challenge as I really didn't care for him.

Sky came home and watch me get dress. After changing three times she finally said that looks better. We left by way of limo and was going to meet him at the restaurant.

At dinner I apologize to them both for my previous behavior and thank them for getting us such a beautiful place. Dillon assured me it was ok, that I deserve the best and from now I'll be treated like royalty while in his presence as you're the mother of the woman I love.

At hearing mother, I cringed.

When he said that my stomach knotted up and a pain went thru my chest. I was hoping neither one of them notice my facial expression. I didn't know what that meant however after hearing those same exact words for the fourth time, I knew I would find out soon. But tonight, I just wanted to enjoy my dinner, and keep peace. So, I sat quietly and enjoyed the ambiance of the restaurant.

Six months living in the townhouse was great. The move was just what I needed.

Dillon was true to his word staying with us for a day or two every other week. I don't know when it changed but every other week became three or four nights a week.

Nine months later I was told he would be moving in. Permanently. My room and patio quickly became my safe haven.

In my mind I wanted to say Ok Mr. Money Bags what happen to the estate you lived in??

As it happens around that time, my Company had just hired new recruits and I would be busy arranging their hiring packages, air fares, houses for the next eight weeks and hiring new trainers. So, I wouldn't be home much.

It didn't hurt that one of the new recruits caught my eye and held my interest. His name was Casper Dupont, tall, chocolate and bald.

CHAPTER THIRTEEN

OVER A PERIOD of a few months, I watched Sky being transformed from his lady/partner to his servant. I wondered if she realizes or noticed the change as I did. Dillon would sit there and she would do whatever it is he wanted done, often time with just a nod of his head.

One evening I watched Dillon sitting at the kitchen table. Sky was in the living room watching television. He called for her to bring him "sparkling" water. Now the water was in the kitchen and all he had to do was get up and get it. Instead Sky was in there in a matter of seconds pouring water into a wine glass and handed it to him.

My instinct was stronger than ever. I'm seeing and hearing all this and I know in my heart something was wrong with this relationship. I'm sure of it. And I still tried to get along with him in spite of all l was seeing.

He was slowly taken ownership of the townhouse which in the beginning was Sky and mine.

He knew I saw the gradual changes in Sky servitude to him as he would often stare at me as though so say, "Say something." Those eyes I once saw as beautiful now appeared black each time he and I stared at each other. I didn't like what was taken place. I could have left at any time but deep down I felt Sky needed me so I stayed.

Sky phone my job one afternoon and announced the three of us would be going to dinner that night. She pleaded with me wear the outfit she laid on my bed as this was a very special occasion. As I held the phone in my hand listening to the dial tone, I was thinking a special occasion? Now what?

Before I finish getting dress, Sky came home alone, which was a shock because they were always together. As I came out of my room, she was right behind me in a beautiful gown Sky said Dillon had gotten dress at the spa. We are to him at the restaurant.

Gage was outside waiting by the limo. I was praying no security escort. God heard my prayer. There were no escort.

We were driven up a steep hill to a restaurant that overlooks the entire city. Regardless to which direction you looked, the city was beautiful as if you were watching a light show. So many colors of lights blinking all at once.

Upon arrival a valet opens the back door of the limo. I felt like I was home watching the awards except there was no red carpet. By the time we reach the door of the restaurant Gage was there with the restaurant door open.

Ok...here I go again...thinking red carpet without the carpet. I was in full alert mode.

The hostess approached us and said, "Mr. Mason was at the table and awaiting our arrival." When she said table, I was expecting a table in a room of people, not a separate area with no one there but us. He even had a waiter and waitress standing by just to serve our table.

Sitting there in tinted glasses, he didn't rise to greet either of us. Instead our chairs were pulled out and napkins placed in our laps. Dillon didn't touch his menu. I watched as Sky ordered for him, then for herself. Lucky for me I got to order what I wanted.

There was small talk made by Dillon. Sky remain quiet and hanging onto his every word...never taken her eyes off him. I had no idea what he was talking about or whom so I continued to enjoy my dinner and wine.

After dinner, champagne was brought out and poured. I refused the champagne and wine was poured into my glass. That feeling I had been having crept up again. I held my breath as I could feel his eyes on me. Whatever was going with those two was about to be revealed.

Dillon looked directly at me and ask for Sky hand in marriage.

I choked on the wine and when I got my coughing under control. I didn't look at him but at Sky. I wanted to see if there was happiness on her face. Instead of her expressing any emotion, she held her head down. I could see her fumbling for something in her hand bag.

Sky spoke at last and said they had already set a date. She showed me this white ring box which held her wedding ring. A very large yellow diamond, which Dillon proudly said with a grin on his face, "Mother its six carat and very rare." She pulled out another ring box which held his band. That band had so many diamonds, I actually laugh as I didn't know men wore that many diamonds. Then I remembered this man had money and the means to do

whatever he wanted. Even wear a cluster of diamonds.

I spoke directly to Dillon, "If the two of you have set a date, why ask me for her hand in marriage?" He replied, "Because she insisted. She also wants you to design her dress. I explained to her I already had arranged a fitting for her and told the designer what I wanted to see her in. But after countless discussions I gave in."

"Now mother I know you design the " working" woman clothes but I have never seen your work, especially a wedding gown. Sky assured me you can do it." He made it sound like I did manual labor.

Sky looked at me with no expression on her face and asked if I would design her the perfect gown for the perfect wedding. I replied, "I would do my best." Dillon placed a card on the table of the designer and stated he wanted the gown to be the way "she" would have designed it. I never touched the card or looked in his direction.

I could feel him starting at me but I never looked his way. I kept my eyes on Sky. Still no expression on her face. Finally, he raised his glass as did Sky and said "Too us." My glass never left the table.

The ride home was very quiet as I had nothing to say to either of them the rest of the evening.

The quiet was very nice and I poured me another glass of wine then another.

Each Day Is Shaped By Big

And

Little Moments

(The Ultimate Checlist For Life)

CHAPTER FOURTEEN

IN THREE WEEKS, I had designed the gown Sky wanted. Another two weeks it was completed and she looked absolutely stunning. This was her day and the bride decision should be considered. Not his designer. Not this time Dillon.

Eight weeks later we flew to the wedding which included Sky and our immediate family. No one was there for Dillon and I asked no question. The vows were exchanged and just like that I had the devil for a son-n-law.

After the wedding Dillon asked again. "May I call you mother?" I replied, "Dillon you may address me as Fiona."

Only three wedding pictures were taking. One with Dillon and Sky, one with Sky alone and the last one with Sky and our family. Dillon refused to be in the family picture. Inside I smiled.

Without me knowing, he had arranged for the dress designer he originally wanted to design a tea length gown for Sky to change into right after the wedding. He starred at me and smiled. I had no expression on my face as I'm sure he was hoping to see anger there. Instead I said, "Sky you look nice."

We walked them to the valet section of the hotel and there waiting for them was a white Rolls Royce and Gage. *What is it with Dillon and white???*

Before getting in the Rolls, Sky handed me an envelope and said, "You and auntie have fun." After they drove away, we looked inside to find twenty (20) one hundred bills. We both laugh and said at the same time "Guilt money."

A year after the wedding, I had to go away on a business trip for 3 weeks.

Upon returning to the townhouse, it looked just like it did before we moved in. Clean and empty. I didn't think a robbery had occurred as the place was too clean.

I went and spoke to the manager. He informed me a moving van had showed up a few days ago, the keys were return by my daughter, and she ask that I give you the security deposit back along with this envelope.

The envelope was in Sky handwriting. Inside was a note telling me they had moved, that my furniture was in storage and it had been paid for six months. Also, inside was check in the amount of five thousand dollars made out to Fiona Grant. No explanation was given. No good bye mom. No, I'm sorry mom. Just the location of the storage and number of the unit 666.

I drove to Phoenix and we sat on her front steps. She didn't know anything was wrong until I showed her the envelope. She read the note twice and offered me her guest room. All I could think about was that Dillon had come in my home, my life and taken what was mind. My only child.

Too angry to cry, I prayed for her safety and comfort for myself.

This Too Shall Pass

Chapter Fifteen

I TOOK THE check and put it with the other unopen envelopes in the storage unit.

I sold my other house with the hope of finding another one soon. Within six months Phoenix and I found a very nice house. With the monies from my other house it allowed me to put down a sizable amount down and didn't have a huge mortgage.

Next on my list was to clean out storage unit 666. I took my time and separate my clothes and furniture I purchased. I was leaving everything Dillon and Sky brought behind in one of the brown boxes or on the floor. That included clothes, shoes, purses, jewelry and the few pieces of furniture they brought. I didn't care what the storage owner would do with it and I didn't care. I wanted no reminders of Beverly Hills and especially of Dillon Mason. However, I made sure I took all the unopen envelopes.

Once I was all moved, I took a month off work to learn the area and enjoy my patio.

I phone Sky, left a message that I had sold the house, and purchased another in another county. I gave her my address; told her I would be keeping the same cell number and hope to hear from her soon. I didn't bother to tell her about all the items I left in the storage unit.

Every day I was hoping she would call. I started calling once a week, then once a month and finally after six months I stopped calling. Praying one day she would reach out to me.

My heart was telling me Sky was gone with Dillon somewhere to some unknown maybe remote location. But I knew my girl and one day she would be back. So, I waited. I had lost my child to the devil but being a true believer, having faith in GOD, I know the devil can't keep what's not his.

Reminiscing back to 2000, when I started to feel things and see signs that something wasn't right, I should have spoken up.

Thanksgiving dinner, seeing him for the first time and speaking with him, I knew something was amiss about this man. But who would have believed me if I spoke my mind?

I talked to my sister about these feelings of guilt and she would say," Girl it's just you being overly concern about your only child. Sky is a smart girl and knows right from wrong."

Well that may be true. But a mother knows what she knows. Sky was in pain.

A year had passed and I had start receiving calls but no one would be there. I knew it was her.

Every other week the same thing. I would say, "Sky its ok. I'm here if you need me."

Six month later she did call and actually spoke. I had to force myself to breathe. To just listen.

She never told me where they were living. Only, "Mom I'm alright" and would hang up before I had a chance to say anything. I could tell from her voice she was lying. She also knew if she stayed on the phone, I would probably ask questions. I didn't want her to withdraw, not call again or hang up so I remain silent. Then a thought occurred to me. She was with Dillon and he was listening are either allowed her to call.

My heart ache because I missed her so much. And yet I had to be very patient or risk losing contact with again.

Chapter Sixteen

TWO MONTHS LATER while sitting in my house the phone rang and when I picked up, said hello, the other person had hung up. I knew it was her again. Was she trying to tell me something?

May of the next year my door rang. When I open the door there stood Sky. I quickly open the screen door and open my arms for her and she came to me willing for only a brief moment. I hated to let her go. Then I looked behind her and understood why she step away so quickly. Her husband was there, still grinning and wearing dark sunglasses.

Dillon push Sky aside as though he was my child. He reached out to grab me but I stepped away and ask them to come in. I looked outside and there was no limo just an ordinary car. I didn't ask questions. I didn't offer any refreshments. I wanted to listen and yes, I had more questions than ever but felt I needed to hear what they had to say.

Sky said, "We just drop by to see your place." And to this day I've never forgotten the words that came from Dillon. "Mother is this what is called the ghetto". I was shocked by his ignorance. But I couldn't ignore that remark. I replied, "No this is my home and it's not the ghetto." (*And this time I shall not be moved*).

A few months after that visit they both appeared at my office. Right behind Dillon was a florist carrying an enormous bouquet of flowers. With a big grin he said, "These are for you mother."

I asked the florist to place the flowers on the corner cabinet. *Because* I was at work with my door open, I whispered, "Don't call me mother. My name is Fiona."

They wanted to take me to lunch and since I had not eaten, I accepted.

Once outside I was looking for the limo, Sky SUV or his fancy car. Instead there was a Hummer parked and knowing Dillon, I knew it was theirs.

I was right. Sky informed me this was hers and that she no longer had the Lincoln. I asked her what happen to the limo, Gage and the other automobiles. Both were quiet. Neither one replied.

What happen next left me with my mouth open. Sky open the back door for Dillon to get in and closed it after he was seated. I opened my door, climbed into the front seat and my mind went to a dark place but I said nothing as Sky got into the driver seat. I looked back at Dillon, he had on dark glasses and was smiling.

We got to the restaurant; the valet opens all doors. Dillon still had on his glasses and now had an even bigger grin on his face. Sky ordered his food then hers. I of course ordered for myself.

All the while my mind went to that dark place which was like an empty hole.

After the table was cleared and I was waiting on my coffee, I looked directly at Sky and asked, "if she was alright?"

She looked at Dillon and he responded, "She's find mother. Probably a little tired from all the driving."

I spoke to him as calmly as I could as we were in public. "Dillon I was asking Sky a question and I would appreciate if you let her speak for herself. And if she is tired from all the driving why don't you drive?" He looked at me, smiled raised his hand for the check and Sky paid the bill.

I was being dismissed or ignored and I dare to venture which one.

Being quiet was over for me. As we waited for the car to arrive, I ask my questions and if he wanted to answer questions then here goes:

1.   What happen to make you move from Beverly Hills?

2.   Why did you think if was ok to put my personal affects in storage?

3.   What on earth were you thinking to leave me a note and a check with the landlord?

4. Where did you two go for almost five years with no communication of any kind?

AND THE BIG QUESTION

5. Why are you here now?

Of course, none of the questions were answered. It was as if I was talking to my self and that made me angry. So angry I could feel the fire raising through me and I felt I needed a time out.

On the ride back to my office Sky never said a word. It was like she had lost her voice. I now knew for sure something was wrong.

Back at my office neither got out. I grabbed Sky hand and kissed it. Dillon just sat in the back seat wearing his dark glasses, smiling looking straight ahead. I hated to see them leave but knew I would see them again.

I gave the flowers to my secretary.

———— ·✦✦✦✦· ————

Still angry when I got home, I was sitting on the patio having a glass of wine. I called Casper and invited him over for wine and a lite dinner. Within the hour we were both enjoying a second bottle. And for some reason I thought of the unopen envelopes I had placed in a box upstairs in my closet.

I went to retrieve the box, return to the patio and placed the box on the table. I removed the top and placed all the envelopes on the table in front of Casper and explain these envelopes contain guilt, shame and love tokens from my daughter and son-n-law.

As I open each envelope, there was cash and checks. The checks that were no longer valid, I put aside to be shredded. Casper did the honor of counting the money as I called it out. Over the years there was a total of fifty thousand dollars in cash and checks.

We each had another glass of wine, place the monies and checks back in the box and I decided it was time to make a deposit. With a toast, Casper agreed.

CHAPTER SEVENTEEN

A YEAR LATER around nine at night, Sky appeared at my house in tears. First thing I looked for were bruises. Satisfied there were none we went to the living room and sat on the sofa. I told her to talk to me and tell me what's wrong.

She laid her head in my lap and cried for almost half an hour. When she finally stops, she said, "Mom it's all gone. We lost it all. You were right the cars, limo and plane were leases. The offices he maintained were what's called virtual office. All gone."

"Dillon is broke mom. The house we were living in was least, the owner sold it and we have to move within thirty days. We have no place to go."

Sky looked at me and I'm sure for answers and or a solution to their problem.

I had four questions:

1. Why were you living in a least house when he claims to have rental properties?

2. What do you mean he lost it all and how?

3. What about his many business he talked about?

4. More importantly how could a man such as Dillon Mason lose everything?

Honestly, I found this hard to believe but…it could be possible. And yet I found myself smiling.

Sky started to repeat herself as though I didn't her the first time. I did. It was Sky who wasn't listening to my questions and of course offered no answers.

After some time had passed and she finished telling me what she wanted me to know, I ask, "Where is Dillon now and why didn't he come with you?"

Mom he had me park two streets over and walk here. I looked at her and said, "You have got to be joking? He had you, his wife walk here in the dark at nine at night while he sits probably in the backseat?" Without a smile on her face she said, "Yes mom."

Her next statements almost cause me a heart attack. She asked if they could move in with me for about six months maybe less until Dillon can straighten all this out. He said it was all a big misunderstanding.

Sky what happen to your common sense?

My mind went into recall mode of the beautiful townhouse we shared in Beverly Hills. How the two of them move out with no warning or regards for me. Although they paid for six months of storage, the sheer thought of even putting my belonging in storage was enough to make me angry all over again, the letter to the manager, note to me with a check in it and silence from Sky for FIVE LONG YEARS!

I didn't allow myself to respond to Sky right away as I was angry at them both. For her being stupid and him just because he was the spawn of the devil and took my child from me. He sent her because he knew I wouldn't say no. *Well played Dillon.*

+ + + + + +

I took this time to make a fresh pot of coffee and poured a cup just for me. Sky had this surprise look on her face as if I should give her an answer right away. I said nothing, drank my coffee and looked at her. Finally, I asked, "Why didn't Dillon come with you and ask me himself if his intention is to stay here?"

She replied, "He knows you don't like him". I responded, "I don't but he is your husband. Go get him so we can all three have a civil conversation."

Once they return, I ask "Dillon if you lost everything what do you plan to do and how are you going to take care of your wife?" He responded, "I still have money put away here and there and can obtain other resources if needed." After that statement I didn't want to know what any of that meant.

Looking at them both I said, "Six months you can move in but your furniture will have to go in storage and not my garage. Month seven if you are a man of your word you **will** be gone."

He looked at me and smiled. I felt a chill. A cold chill. The devil was moving into my house.

I would come home from work; he would be sitting watching television. Sky had beginning waiting on him, driving him where ever he wanted to go as he sat in the back seat with those dark glasses on.

They were living in my house but never received mail. It was like they didn't exist.

Sky and I no longer had mother - daughter talks as he was always within ear shot, always listening, always answering if I ask her a question.

My questions were always the same to him, what really happen to all your wealth and business? I never got answers just that grin I had come to hate. I sometimes wonder did he ever own anything.

I saw Dillon as the devil wearing a smile that covered up the ugliness in his heart. I'll always believe once he had lost "everything" that he formulated a plan. He knew I would do anything for Sky so he manipulated her into getting what he wanted including my money.

It was Sky who always came to me when money was needed. She went from can I borrow five hundred, to can I borrow one, two or five thousand dollars. Each time with a promise to pay it back. I had no problem lending the money as it was theirs. It was the monies they had been putting in envelopes for me for one reason or another. So, it didn't matter that it was never paid back.

When their money plus the interest that had accumulated ran out then it became a problem. Whenever Sky ask for loan, I wanted to know why but never got an answer. This time they needed to borrow ten thousand dollars.

Having said no for the first time, I felt guilty and wrote out a check. But before I handed it over, I asked Sky and Dillon what they did with all the money I loaned them? With that grin of his he replied, "I'm making business transactions to get us out of here."

I was not satisfied with the answer given and said so. He walked away and Sky right behind him. They went upstairs without my check which was the last of my personal savings.

I wanted a better answer than what he offered as I knew it was a lie. He never left the house. And when they did it was to the gym or spa. Sky didn't go anywhere but to the store and back. Other than that, he was always in "his" chair watching television.

After that I was treated as though I was a stranger in my own home. I never saw them when I came home but heard him reading his Bible. I can only imagine her sitting their obediently. I didn't like who she had become and blamed Dillon.

A few weeks had gone by and they both started coming down stairs, always together. Sky started talking to me and he would sit in the same chair in front of the television wearing a grin, dressed in a suit without a tie but he had on his diamond cuff links. Sky dressed in the same color as he but now they had no were to be.

Dillon approached me as I was drinking coffee on the patio one evening and asked again to borrow ten thousand dollars and of course the same old question from me. Why?

I didn't wait for an answer instead I said, "You've been at my house well over a year and it's time for you to go. So yes, I'll loan you the money. Maybe it will help your business ventures speed up the process of whatever you're trying to accomplish and of course move you out."

Without looking at him I went into the kitchen, in my purse and pulled out my check book. I wrote the check and laid it on the table. I could feel his cold eyes on me as he picked up the check and walked back upstairs. No thank you. No nothing.

CHAPTER EIGHTEEN

ONE EVENING WHEN I return from work, Dillon suggested we all go to dinner. Sky was not in an evening gown but look just as elegant. Dillon always dressed nice even when sitting in front of the television. And much to my surprise I was not asked to change clothes.

The routine of going somewhere was always the same. Sky open the back door for Dillon, and of course he was wearing dark glasses and smiling.

The restaurant we dined at that evening everyone knew him. The valet was given twenty dollars for parking the Hummer. The doorman was given ten dollars. The hostess was given twenty dollars just for seating us. The manager came out personally to meet him and said, "Mr. Mason so nice to see you again." A hundred-dollar bill was placed in his hand. Dillon sat at the head of the table and the mai*tre d ask if he wanted the usual. He said,

"Yes, and bring a bottle of sparkling water and a plain glass of water with ice for my mother in law." Once he returned with the waters, he was given ten dollars.

Dinner was brought out so was a bottle of wine. This person was given twenty dollars. I thought this was over excessive but said nothing. After Dillon tasted his wine, he looked at Sky nodded his head and she drink hers. After dinner was over, he left a fifty-dollar tip on the table.

The hummer was brought around, more money was given out and he of course got in the back seat still with the glasses on looking straight ahead telling Sky where to go for his coffee and dessert. Sky felt the need to tell me Dillon never has coffee and desert where he eats. I replied, "I remembered."

I was starting to believe she had been brain washed or she was terrible afraid of him. One thing for sure she had replaced Gage as his chauffer.

I started paying more attention to what was going on when I was with them. There were so many signs something was not right. Only I couldn't figure it out. What I did know for sure Sky was no longer happy and it had nothing to do with "everything being gone." No, it was more than that. Her total behavior and demeanor had changed.

Dillon behavior had become so erratic that it started to worry me. He would read the Bible daily, not that anything was wrong with it, but I had never seen him pick up a Bible before. He started teaching Sky the Bible and when I heard him preaching in the house, I thought he had gone mad.

He asked me on several occasion to join them in taking Communion. I always refused. Next, he was wearing a clergy collar around his neck. Always riding in the back seat with dark glasses, now wearing a clergyman collar and a Bible next to him.

Six months turned into six years year and they were still living in my home!

Dillon was still preaching in the house, doing his Communion, going to the gym and spa daily with Sky being the chauffer.

No one was working in the house but me. And looking at him made me want to vomit and shake some sense in to Sky.

She did buy food for the house and prepared his food as if in a restaurant. He would sit at the table with a cloth napkin, place setting, and two glasses, one for water and the other for wine. One day out of curiosity I ask Sky, "Why is there only one place setting when there is three of us?" Her response was Dillon prefers to dine alone. Now after dinner he had coffee at home, upstairs where Sky took it to him on a tray.

She took her meals with me which made me happy as we were alone. As soon as I started talking, we could hear him coming down the stairs. I believe he thought I was going to ask Sky about his business. What he didn't know I no longer cared about him or his affairs. But poor Sky wouldn't say anything not even nod her head. So, she ate in silence. Always with me talking.

One Saturday while Dillon was upstairs taking a nap, I asked Sky if she was enjoying the gym and spa. She said, "Mom I sit in the car and wait for Dillon." For the second time I actually saw her crying. Without looking at me she said," Mom I'm afraid and don't know what to do."

My baby was hurting. Something was terribly wrong. I knew what she had just told me took a lot of courage. One day and I pray soon - she would tell me everything.

One morning while in the kitchen preparing to go to the office, Dillon came into the kitchen and said, "Mother I'm so happy we're here." My response, "how much longer do you plan to be happy here? When are you going to get a job?"

What he said next I could feel anger coming thru me. With that devilish grin of his, "I sent Sky out this morning to look for a job as I have the Word to spread among the people. That is my true calling mother. I'm a man of God." I stood there staring at him for the longest time saying nothing. I just stood there as though time had frozen.

When I did trust myself to speak. I said very calmly, "Dillon you are not a man of God but the devil in human form. What kind of man sends his wife out to look for a job while you sit all day doing nothing? You are power hunger and very controlling. You have no friends so just who are you spreading the Word to Dillon?"

He said nothing. Not one word. He just started laughing as though I said something funny. As quickly as he started laughing, he stopped and grinned at me. Turned and went to "his" chair and turn on the television.

Chapter Nineteen

ANOTHER YEAR HAD gone by with only Sky and I going to work.

For Christmas Dillon gave each of us a mink coat. *(Now where did the money come from?)*

Sky was very happy with her new coat. It was the third one he had given her since they met. My coat remained in the box on the floor. He left the room and return wearing a full-length fur coat the same color as Sky.

Before I left the room I, couldn't hold my tongue any longer, I ask Dillon where did he get the money to buy three fur coats? I know the job Sky had wasn't enough to pay for even one. I wasn't expecting an answer but he did reply. His response was, "Mother just be happy and enjoy your gift." I kept walking but with a cold chill. My coat still in the box on the floor.

Later that same evening, Sky had made reservation for a restaurant in Beverly Hills and they both were dressed in the same colors and had their new coats in hanger bags. I wore one of my own coats and paid no attention to either of them when they suggested I wear my fur.

That fur was still on the floor where I left it that morning.

Before reaching the restaurant, she stops and they put on their furs. I shook my head and looked straight ahead. At the restaurant there was a line of people waiting to get in but as usual, there was no problem with the Mason family getting in. His door was open first, money exchanged hands. He was greeted at the door, money exchanged hands, their mink coats and my coat were taken, and money exchanged hands.

I overheard the hostess say, "Mr. Mason your table is ready for you and your party." Sky ordered for him, he said nothing the entire evening and never took off those dark glasses.

Once back home, I asked Dillon if he was hiding from someone. I caught a brief glimpse of Sky shaking her head and the expression was one of fear.

Dillon smiled and said, "Mother it's none of your business. Sky it is time for us to retire for the evening." I spoke directly to Dillon and said, "As long as you live in my house, everything you do Dillon Mason is my business. I don't know what's going on and not sure I want to know but if it involves my house or Sky, I have a right to ask and know." He turned and smiled at me. Held out his hand to Sky and said, "Come."

She looked back at me and mouthed; I love you mom. My face became warm and I didn't realize those were tears rolling down my face.

A week later Dillon approached me, smiled then hugged me from behind. I could feel the negative energy flowing from him. He said, "Mother you've made me so happy that we are all together. You are the family I never had. Sky and I are going to give you at least six grandchildren. Would that make you happy?"

I looked at him as though seeing him for the first time. Does he really think children will make me like him or solve their problem? Did he not remember what was said two weeks ago?

Instead of answering his question, I asked, "Where was Sky". I had not seen her since last night. He said, "She's not well and was resting." I wanted to see for myself. As I headed to the stairs, he blocked my way and said in a loud voice, "*she is resting and doesn't want to be disturb.*"

And hour later Sky comes into the kitchen and says she had not been feeling well. I asked her did you're not feeling well have anything to do with the conversation Dillon and I had previously? She never answered.

As she was leaving the kitchen, I said, "if he is hurting you – call 911. But if you can call me, I'll be there a lot quicker."

She went quietly back upstairs. I turned around to see her nod her head and wipe her face.

I heard a second pair of footsteps go upstairs and knew he had been listening. Good Dillon. I hope your heard me well.

A Storm Is Coming

CHAPTER TWENTY

SOMETIME LATER THE next day they both came into the dining room. Dillon with that devilish grin and the coldest that followed. Sky standing by him. She said how happy they both were to be here with me. Dillon said it feels like old times when we lived in Beverly Hills.

Ok he is certifiable crazy. The good times in Beverly Hills lasted only for a short time. Then I was left behind, but who knows maybe he was speaking of his good times in his Beverly Hills estate, when he had lots and lots of money.

I looked at them both and said, "What are referring too? You both left without a good bye, moved my things into storage and left me a check. Is that Dillon what you are referring to feel like old times?"

Dillon started laughing and walked away with Sky right behind him.

A short time later Dillon came back downstairs and found me sitting on the patio reading a book. He took the book from my hand and stared at me. His eyes appeared black and again I felt a chill. It seems like each time he came around me I was always cold.

I didn't like being looked down on or at a disadvantage, so I stood up to stare back at him. Before he could speak, I told him in a calm voice, "Dillon you are interrupting my quiet time, please hand me back my book."

He just continued to stare at me all the while holding my book. I was not going to be defeated by this man so we just started at each other.

Eventually he placed the book on the table and turn to leave. With his foot in the door I said, "Dillon I don't know who or what you are but I'm not Sky and not afraid of you." He turns to look at me and

74

said in that voice I never heard, "**You should be Fiona**." This time the it seems the chilled entered by body and wouldn't go away.

As I sat there thinking about what just happen, my cell phone rang and I jumped. I quickly answered and was glad to hear Casper voice. I told him to come over and have coffee so we could talk.

When he arrived, I made us lunch and we talked. After lunch I was telling him the things that had been taking place and the changes going on with Sky and Dillon.

He just looked at me in disbelief. He assured me it was all in my mind. That there was no such thing as the devil living in my house.

When he left, I remembered this verse from the Bible:

It is GOD who arms me with strength and makes my way perfect. Psalm 18:32 NKJV

*For some strange reason I knew I would need **HIS** protection*

CHAPTER TWENTY-ONE

ANOTHER SIX MONTHS had gone by, there still here and everything appeared to be normal only it wasn't normal.

Sky and I decided to go play bingo. I found it strange that Dillon wanted to stay home.

As we were leaving bingo that night, she called Dillon to inquire if he wanted food or coffee as we would be stopping before coming home. He didn't want anything not even coffee. Dillon refusing coffee was strange but she thought nothing of it. I had a bad feeling as he loved coffee just as much if not more than myself.

As we pulled into the garage, the lights were on and the back door that lead into the house was unlock. When we entered the house, I felt that chill again. My intuition told me something was wrong. I felt strange. A weird feeling came over me. I became restless and I mention all of this to Sky. She laughs and said, "Oh mom. You and those premonitions."

As she proceeded upstairs, I gave her a big hug and said good night. She looked back at me and said, "Good night mom. I had fun tonight."

I went to my room, and for the first time since they moved in, I left the door open. I laid on the bed with my clothes on including my shoes. Still having all these strange feelings and now feeling restless.

Almost within minutes, I heard Dillon raising his voice calling Sky everything but Sky in a very strange voice. The same voice I heard on the patio a few days ago. Upon hearing Dillon go on and on and

Sky being quiet I was getting worried but didn't leave my room. Instead I sat up on the side of the bed.

Then I heard her say, "Stop! You're hurting me." Then quiet.

Still in my room I listen again and it was quiet.

Minutes later I heard Sky say, "You should leave Dillon or I'll call the police."

I head Dillon say, "I'm sorry. I didn't mean to hurt you. Let's pray."

I was thinking to myself - they are having a disagreement; he has caused pain and he wants to pray?

Time for a cup of coffee.

About two hours had passed and he started yelling again. This time calling her whore being born of a bitch. He kept saying you and all your friends are whores. Any woman who goes out alone with her mother as you say to play bingo, which I don't believe, should die and go to hell.

A few minutes later another outburst.

Now you expect me to believe you and your girlfriends are planning a four-day trip? Sky you have no girlfriends. I saw to that personally. Didn't you ever wonder why they never came around? Money can buy anything especially when offered enough. Did you ever wonder why I had you to drop out of school? I, Dillon Mason, made you who you are. Not your precious bitch of a mother. And yet you're still ignorant. Or do you think I'm stupid?

No respectful woman leaves her husband to go anywhere alone, with her mother and especially not on a four-day trip with girlfriends, in which you don't have.

Sky asked him, "Why can't a woman go somewhere without her husband? What's wrong with-it Dillon? His response shocked me. It's the law. My law!

All of a sudden I heard this strange voice again saying, "I know you and mother didn't go play bingo. I know you were with another man or out there looking for one. I think we need to have a baby right now. I don't want to wait any longer."

Sky said, "NO! No kids! Not now! Not ever! Not with you Dillon. Your evil and mean now leave me alone."

Dillon replied, "I knew you were a whore." I wouldn't want you to have my child. You are not worthy to have my child. You're just like all the rest of the women out there unclean including your precious mother.

I had heard enough of that kind of talk. I got off my bed and headed toward the front of house. I went to the stairs and called Dillon and got no response.

"Dillon, I know you hear me. All right you be quiet and listen. That's probably better. But listen well, as you know I don't like to repeat myself. I've had enough of your loud talking and being disrespectful in my house. It's one thing for you and Sky to disagree. But when you started using that type of language and calling your wife a whore. And the audacity to call me something other than my name? Well mister you have gone a little too far!

"I don't like getting in whatever you two are arguing about as I don't know what it's about nor do I want to know. Just keep your hands off each other before it goes too far."

"And Dillon remember this today and going forward this is my house and that's my law. If you don't like my law, you can always leave. Just you Dillon and don't leave a forwarding address. Sky stays here."

After returning to my room my bones became cold and I found myself sweating. I had a feeling of uneasiness that something more was coming. Something very **very** bad.

Dillon had started his own private war. With Sky and myself his sworn enemies.

Now I know the devil was truly in my house. Upstairs in the bedroom.

It became quiet upstairs. I did something I never do and that's *assumed*. Therefore, by assuming it was over, I allowed myself to sleep.

Time Allows You To See A Person For

Whom They Really

Are

CHAPTER TWENTY-TWO

I WAS AWAKENED by a faint scream, "Momm…mie" so I sat up in bed and heard it again "Momm…mie". I ran up the stairs and stopped. Stopped in disbelief at what I was seeing.

I couldn't believe that could be my child laying on the floor with her head bobbing up and down. Not realizing I was looking at blood, I kept thinking why is all that that black stuff coming from Sky mouth? I must have stood there for a minute or two but it seems like hours had pass as I watch Dillon with his foot in her back continue to strike her in the head. With tremendous blows her head would come up off the floor and then back down.

I actually thought I was dreaming and realize this was no dream! Dillon was killing my child!

I screamed at him to stop hitting her. To get off her and leave my house. He slowly turns around with those black eyes, looks at me and said "oh so where am I supposed to go?" I replied, "I don't care but you have to get out now or I'm calling the police."

Dillon takes his foot off Sky and kicks her so hard in her side until she curls up like a fetus and moans, "Oh God. Mom help me". He starts off down the hallway laughing.

As I'm kneeling down to check Sky, I didn't see Dillon when he turned around in the hall and headed back into the bedroom. Before I knew what was happening, he grabs me from behind and throws me behind Sky which caused me to break the mirrored closet door.

I remember I bounced from the shattered glass of the closet and hitting my head on the edge of the night stand. I could hear Sky quietly saying," Stop don't hurt my mom".

I didn't realize the blood that was on me was my blood from the gash on my forehead. The pain I felt in my head was unbearable. Dillon came toward me again. This time with his fist. All I could do was put up my arm to ward off the blows but they just kept coming. I heard something crack and couldn't move my arm. It felt so heavy. I could taste blood and no longer see out of my left eye. I felt helpless and could barely move. There were no tears. Just pain.

I heard a muffle sound *"you're killing my mom"*. The sound of Sky voice gave me enough strength to inch my way to her and gently nudge her with my foot. I said, "Baby if you can stand up, run, don't look back and get help. I'm ok. I will find you."

Sky could barely stand up. She fell down twice. Dillon took advantage of this and once again kicked her hard in the side causing more pain. She stops moving but somehow manage to make it downstairs.

I stood up holding my side, my arm felt as if I was carrying something heavy. I said in a clear but loud voice **STOP!** Leave her alone Dillon. You want to hit a woman come hit me. And to my surprise those black eyes headed back up the stairs and with his fist hits me in the face. I fell backward.

Moaning and crying softly, I managed to see Sky roll down the second flight of stairs. When I heard her hit the mirror, I knew it wouldn't be long before she is out the front door open. I could hear Sky screaming, "Help us! Help us please! Call the police!"

Then quiet.

No screaming from Sky. She was safe. I knew the police would be here soon. I tried to smile but was in so much pain. I silently prayed as I heard Dillon laughing.

Neither of us knew if the police were on the way and what happen next still gives me cold chills.

I was still laying on the floor, he comes to me, straddles me so tight I could feel his ankles pressing my side and started punching me in the face and head with his fist.

The he stopped and walked away.

I heard moaning and realize it was me still in the door of the bedroom. Too sore to move.

I don't know when the hitting stopped or where Dillon went. But I knew I had to get up and get out the house.

Struggling to stand up, I headed out the bedroom door. That's when I saw Dillon coming around the bed with a ceramic lamp wrapping the cord around the base. I was thinking what is he doing. The bulb is still in there. He starts hitting me with the base of the lamp until I sank to the floor. Again, he straddles my body so I couldn't move. The pain was so unbearable until I felt nothing but the blows and blood flowing.

He continued hitting me saying "I'm not going anywhere".

He keeps hitting me till the base of the lamp shattered. I prayed the hitting was over until I felt something sharp digging into the top of my head. I realize it was the part of the lamp that holds in light bulb. The bulb was broken and this mad man was digging the silver part of the blub into the top of my head.

I was trying to get away from him as he grabs the back of my shirt until it rips into and my back is expose. He steps on me as if I was not a person. And maybe in his distorted mind I wasn't.

He was the devil and that night anyone that got in his was going to be hurt. I was still on my back and in so much pain it was hard to move and breath. He grabbed me my head, bent down and said "Mother can you hear me". I just moan and then he hit me again.

Finally, it was quiet in the bedroom. I could hear Dillon down the hallway laughing.

I manage to crawl down the stairs to the first landing and thought I was safe from Dillon. I looked in the mirror and saw him at the top of the stairs holding a vase. I crawled down the last two steps just in time to watch the vase shatter the mirror and see pieces of mirror falling onto the floor.

In only seconds he reached the bottom level and started stomping me in the back. Then I heard a crack. I heard the front door open and felt myself being dragged out. I felt the cold concrete as my head was pushed down. Then a few sharp kicks in the side.

More laugher from Dillon.

The pain had left my body. It was numb. There were no tears. I didn't know if I was alive or dead.

I was waiting for a hit, kick or something. When nothing came, I managed to get up on one knee but not for long. I fell face down. After several falls I laid there on the cold concrete. I pushed myself up and the pain was back with a vengeance. I tried again and again to get up but each time falling. Each time worse than the other.

When I finally managed to get up, I couldn't stand up straight but was bent over. For the first time I cried for myself.

Silently I prayed, "LORD help me find my child in the darkness and the quiet". Then I fell down again this time on my knees. I heard laughter and just knew it was from Dillon. But as I listened it was coming from a distance.

I looked to the left and right and saw people looking but no one was moving. I notice four men standing, drinking, pointing and laughing my way. As the laughter continued, I prayed Dillon was gone.

After three or four tries of trying to get up again I headed toward the school area. Somehow, I knew that's the direction Sky would have chosen.

————————— ·+·++·+·· —————————

That night was like a movie in slow motion and main characters was Dillon Mason as the devil, Skylar and Fiona Grant as the victims.

————————— ·+·++·+·· —————————

I remember being tired and noticing the street lights were on. I saw folks on the sidewalk looking and not moving.

I could feel blood running down my face. Because of the laugher I heard, it must have been funny seeing a woman limping and falling down on the sidewalk screaming, "Has anyone seen my daughter? Has anyone seen my daughter? Which way did she go?"

More laughter.

Dogs barking.

Chapter Twenty-Three

I COULD MAKE out two figures standing in a driveway and didn't know if I was imagining things because of the severe blows to my head or if I was really seeing someone. As I got closer to the two figures standing under the street light, my mind was racing and my heart was beating so fast. But I kept walking toward them and discovered they were both men. They just stood there, hands to their side. One of the men held up his hand and said "Stop!"

Instead of stopping I kept limping forward and said, "I'm looking for my child. Have you seen my daughter?" It never occurred to me they didn't know my daughter. Both looked at me and shook their head. One of them spoke, "No we haven't seen anyone tonight just you."

My knees gave way and I fell flat on my face. One of the men reached down and helps me up, takes off his shirt and puts it around me.

I looked down at myself. Blood now coming from various parts of my body. I notice I had on a bra, jeans badly stain with blood and no shoes.

The laughter I previously heard had stopped.

Someone shouted, "That man has a gun, call the police."

I felt myself been dragged, pushed toward and behind large trash binds at another house. The man who had given me his shirt looked down at me and whispered, "Sshhh. Stay behind the trash can and don't come out until we come for you or the police."

All the while he was talking to me, I was thinking where is Sky. I have got to find her and get her to the hospital. Then I remembered someone had shouted that man has a gun.

I heard that crazy laugher and knew it was Dillon. I was thinking when did he get a gun?

Lots of shots fired.

More shots fired then laughter,

Then another shot.

Then another shot. It seems the shooting went on forever.

I could hear people screaming.

Dogs barking.

I could hear glass shattering as the bullets hit windows. Whenever a car or car window was hit, alarms went off.

There were so many shots fired, I became afraid Dillon would find me and finish the job he tired earlier and that was to kill me.

I was praying whoever lived in the house would come out and offer me safety. Instead I saw the lights go out. And I understood. No one was coming. No one but Dillon to find me and Sky.

Dillon kept shooting, laughing and calling Sky and mother.

Police sirens were getting closer. But the shooting continue as though Dillon didn't hear the sirens.

I recognize the voice as one of the men who was standing there previously say, "Hey man you shot my brother."

I closed my eyes and starting humming gospel songs to myself.

More shots fired. More laughter from Dillon. He asks where was the young woman and the old one.

Dogs barking.

The shooting started again, broken glass and car alarms.

More shots.

People screaming.

Dillon laughing and calling Sky and mother.

More shots.

Dogs barking.

The sound of police sirens and blue lights were on the street. A helicopter overhead with search lights.

The shooting stopped.

Dillon must have saw the bright lights from helicopter. I heard from somewhere, "This is the police. Drop your weapon!"

When all got quiet. Only the barking of the dogs could be heard.

I crawled from behind the trash can and could see the back of Dillon running toward the house. I saw him point a gun to the ground and another was across his shoulder.

The street was now lined with police cars. People standing on their lawns.

There was a shot from the corner house. My house. Dillon was shooting at the police. They were shooting back. This lasted for what seems like hours but in real time it was only a few minutes.

I started to cry and pushed myself back down to the ground. No longer hidden behind the trash cans that belong to the people who turn the lights out.

I prayed for my daughter where ever she was and that she be safe and alive through all this.

I was awakened by smelling salt and in the back of an ambulance. I saw an EMT sitting next to me taking my vital signs and calling out info to another sitting across from me writing on a clip board. Before they could finish, I wanted to know if anyone has found my daughter, Skylar. They just kept talking and reading out numbers as though I had not said a word. I scream, **"Have you found my daughter?"**

The EMTs looked at each other and I knew something was wrong. Although badly injured, I knew I needed to be treated and at the same time I needed to get away from them to go look for Sky.

A police officer came to speak with me asking questions I wasn't ready to answer. I just wanted to know if Sky was found and if she was ok.

It appeared everyone had an agenda or protocol to follow. I didn't. I just wanted to know about my child. Nothing else at that moment matter. Especially Dillon Mason who I heard was held up in my house.

I heard SWAT was on the way.

No one was listening to me when I ask about Sky, refuse to answer or just ignored the crazy half naked woman bleeding. I thought that's ok folks, I'll go find Sky myself. The street is not big. Not thinking of my own injuries, misjudging the height of the ambulance and forgot the pain I was feeling, I remove the oxygen from my face, got up from the cot, pushed past the EMT who was saying something that didn't have the word young lady, her daughter or Sky in the sentence.

By the time I reach the back door of the ambulance and step down, I fell to the ground HARD. Not able to get up, the EMT helped me sit on the back step of the ambulance and this time I was given something for the pain. I was warned not to move as I was going to be transported to the hospital as soon as the police officer ask me a few more questions.

From a distance I heard, "We have a young woman badly beaten send the paramedics to this location now." I knew they had found her and I started crying. Sky had been found and would be receiving medical treatment.

I couldn't see when they brought her out from wherever she had been because policemen were standing in front of me. They stepped aside and that's when I saw her strapped to a gurney. She was unconscious. The EMTs were speaking very rapidly, "Her pulse is very weak! We are losing her!

No pulse!

Paddles! Stand back!

I watched as they shocked her and it seems like she jumped up in midair and back down. The monitor was still the same with a slow beeping sound.

Again, I heard, "Paddles! Stand back! We got a faint pulse! LET'S MOVE!

I actually saw the blue line I've seen so much on television and again heard slow beeping sounds. I knew this was not good. What I heard next made me scream. "She's, CODING....WE HAVE GOT TO MOVE NOW!"

I watched as they drove away with Sky and I wanted Dillon dead.

I should have been in the next ambulance. But I wasn't going anywhere. My child is dying or possible dead.

AND Dillon was going to pay.

I no longer felt pain. I had no more tears. I actually felt nothing. My heart was racing and killing Dillon was on my mind.

He would die or I would.

The Storm Came

And It

Was Mother

Chapter Twenty-Four

❦

I SAW SEVERAL people had been shot and driven away in ambulances. As each one passed, I prayed for them silently. The two good Samaritans that helped me had been shot and taken away by ambulances.

I had no more tears or fear. My body should have been sore but I felt nothing.

I could hear the EMT talking to me but his voice fell on a death ears. They were demanding I go to the hospital to be treated for my wounds and further testing.

I knew my rights and refuse to go to the hospital. I knew my injuries were bad but not yet. I requested to sign a release of liability form.

I willed myself to ignore the pain that racked my entire body, my wrist was very limp and I knew my arm was broken. Yet I felt nothing but pure anger and knew I had to face Dillon no matter what. He had to pay for what he did to Sky.

It was time to show Dillon Mason a real MOTHER.

I saw an officer go over the ambulance I just left and he spoke to the EMT. They showed him papers, the officer shook his head and requested they not move.

Another officer walked over and informed me, the gunman was held up in my house and it wasn't safe for me to be here. He pointed to the ambulance at the corner saying that one was for me. But I knew what needed to be done and I was not afraid to do it and getting in the back of an ambulance was not it.

The officer looked at me and I was smiling. He asks if I was ok. I said, "I'm find. My child was in that first ambulance and had to be shocked back to life twice and then it may or may not have worked.

The man that shot up the street and wounded people is held up in my house. And you ask if I'm ok? Yes, officer, I'm find. How about you? You ok? You still waiting on SWAT to get a strategy together before they break down my door?"

He looked at me and replied, "Ma'am we'll soon have the man in custody."

The two scenario that played in mind were:

1. Dillon would be taken into custody, turn on the charm, hire a lawyer and be free.

2. He would die tonight

I don't remember walking toward my house or speaking to anyone after that. I had one mission and that was to get back into my house and face Dillon.

I kept hearing the word **CODE**. I was more determined than ever to face the devil. Oh yeah, I was going back into my house.

Before anyone knew I was missing, I headed across the lawn. Every few steps I took I was falling but somehow catching myself and kept walking. After the third time I did fall on the ground and a voice inside my head said stand up Fiona and keep moving toward the house.

At last, I was at the front door. As I put my hand on the door knob I heard a police yelling, "Stop her! She can't go in there! The suspect has a gun!"

Now I'm laughing hysterical. They call him a suspect. I call him the devil. **And my child has coded!**

*Yeah though I walk the val-
ley of shadows*

of death, I will fear no evil;

for thou art with me;

they rod and thy

staff comfort me.

Psalm 23:4

For I am the LORD your
God who takes hold

of your right hand says
to you, Do not fear;

I will help you.

Isaiah 41:13

CHAPTER TWENTY-FIVE

I COULD HEAR him upstairs moving around so I called his name. He answered as though nothing had happen and said, "Yes mother." Holding onto the banister and climbing the stairs I kept thinking I should feel more pain. I'm bleeding, my hands are swollen, my head, back, side, chest and feet hurt.

Before reaching that last step, I was met with a big foot that kicked me hard enough that I fell backward down the stairs bumping into what was left of the mirror at the foot of the stairs and rolled down the last two steps.

Before I knew what was happening Dillon was kicking me everywhere including my face. I was so disoriented that I didn't have time to think or at least shield my face.

All of a sudden, he stopped and was saying something that I couldn't understand. I took advantage of that time and stood up to face him. I only had one good eye but saw him clearly and I heard laughter. I realize the laughter was coming from me.

I felt his fist hit me in the face. I heard a crack and spit out blood. As he prepared to hit me again, I manage to dodge the blow. I remember my brothers saying hit down low. And that's what I did. I put all the strength I had left and hit him hard enough to knock him down.

He stayed their holding himself and it was my turn to kick. And kick was what I did. Down low. Then I started laughing again. I just kept hitting and kicking all the while screaming you killed my baby. I started laughing again and now he was shielding himself from my kicks.

Finally, I stopped and was thinking I need a cup of coffee.

I believe I was hysterical, **or** was I??

I walked away from Dillon as he was holding himself, then I saw him feeling his face. He started laughing that sinister laugh.

I stopped. Went back over to him, stood over him as he had done to me and when he moved, I brought my foot down on that beautiful face of his as hard as I could. He said, "Bitch you broke my nose." I never said a word but walked away toward the kitchen looking for something to hurt or that would kill Dillon.

My pain had turn to pure rage. Yes "Mother" had turned into a real mother of a beast. Dillon had no idea of the love I had for my child. I would have swum a river of snot if that what it would take to protect her. So, bring it on Dillon. Mother is ready.

There was so much blood running down my face and out my mouth. My eye had swollen some time ago and was completely closed. I didn't care I wanted to kill this man. ***My house. My rules.***

I heard pounding at the door - THIS IS THE POLICE – OPEN UP!

Ignoring the knock at the door, Dillon grab me from behind and toss me onto the dining table and I rolled on the floor. In two giant strides he was hitting me again and this time I wasn't shielding myself against the blows. I was fighting back for all I was worth.

I was so mad, spitting out blood and a few back teeth. I said, "You hit like a girl," and I started laughing. He hit me again and I kept laughing. This time it was he who looked at me and said in a calm voice, "Mother I'm going to pray for you and ask GOD to forgive you."

To forgive me? You take your bible and pray for your own soul.

All the while I'm saying this, he had the telephone cord in his hand then suddenly around my neck. I felt him pulling it tighter and tighter and saying die. Die like your precious daughter and you two can be together. Then that awful laugh of his.

I know now what the scripture means, ***Psalms 121 NIV***, *I lift up my eyes to the hills – where does my help come from? My help comes from the LORD.*

I had strength to hit him harder than ever until he releases the cord from around my neck. I told Dillon I'm not dying tonight by your hands. And the fight continue as I was not running from him. He wanted a mother…he got one!

CHAPTER TWENTY-SIX

※

I DIDN'T HEAR the door has it crashed.

Both Dillon and I saw SWAT at the same time. Then I heard freeze!

He ran upstairs and I heard the door slam shut. I just laid there too tired to move. I looked up and there were policeman, guns and men in black gear that read SWAT.

A policeman grabs me, pulled me outside where another grabs me and wrap a blanket around my shoulders. Then EMT's examining me again. Before the door to the ambulance closed, I saw this strange little robot going into the house.

I heard the siren of the ambulance and knew this time they were taken me to the hospital. I could feel what they were doing and hear what they were saying. It seems like they've done this before. One of the EMTs was saying they need to stop the bleeding and starting calling out numbers again. I felt the sting of a needle. The last thing I remember, Dillon was still alive.

I remember waking up in a room with a doctor, nurses and police officers. I was on oxygen and hooked up to an IV. I kept looking around the room and notice in the corner Phoenix was crying. So, I surmise I was not dreaming or dead. I kept checking my surroundings and couldn't speak because of a tube down my throat.

The doctor notice I was awake and request that the tube be remove.

The man sitting in a chair next to my bed said he was the detective assign to my case and had a few questions for me. He asked if I knew what happen tonight. I shook my head up and down. He said before leaving my home they found my purse and wallet. The wallet contained my emergency contact so they called my sister.

He explains that pictures had been taken of me when I arrive at Emergency Care for his report. I asked to see them and felt my body go numb. That was not me. No way!

I had questions of my own like how long have I been here? Where is my daughter? Is she alive?

The doctor informed me, I had been in Emergency Care for six hours. My daughter was taken to a Trauma Center because of her injuries. He didn't know the prognosis of her condition only that they were severe.

As I begin removing the cover, the doctor said, "Ms. Grant, you are in no shape to be discharged and we still have a few more test to run."

He proceeded to give me details of what they had done while I was in the Emergency Care Unit.

1. They had to release the blood that had form in my eye by cutting it as my left eye was swollen completely shut.

2. They removed pieces of glass and debris from my head by shaving the top of my head.

3. They remove glass and concrete that was embedded in my face, forehead, then stitched my face and forehead and that I would have bruises for a few days.

4. An MRI was taken of my entire body to detect if there were fractions or broken bones. Sadly, he said, "You have minimal damage to your brain, a hairline factor to the back of your skull, left arm and wrist broken, 2 broken ribs, fractured chest and your knee is busted."

If they told all this to Phoenix, and I'm sure they did, that's why she was crying.

I was listening and understood all that was being said but I wanted out of their as I had to find Sky.

I thanked the doctor and asked when can I be released? He looked at me and wanted to know if I fully understood what he had just said. I assured him I did and would have all that treated, fixed or repaired when I find my daughter and know that she is alive.

Not realizing how sedated I was, I attempted to get out of bed and hit the floor hard rolling over in pain. I could feel the IV as it tore thru my skin. The nurse helped me back into bed and said, "The meds should wear off in another hour." I looked at the nurse, the doctor and the detective now standing in the corner and said, "I don't have an hour. I need to be with my daughter. NOW!"

I felt a prick in my arm and saw the nurse as he walked away. Then blackness.

CHAPTER TWENTY-SEVEN

✦

WHEN I WOKE up Phoenix was sitting by my bed. That same detective was sitting in the corner on his cell and writing on a pad.

When he noticed I was awake, he brought his chair over to the other side of the bed.

He informed me that upon entering my home, they found Mr. Mason in one of the bedrooms upstairs. He was sitting in a chair near the window and unfortunately, he had killed himself. I asked, "How and with what?" He said, "Mr. Mason shot himself with a semi-automatic weapon which caused half his head to be blown away."

The body was still in the room where it happens and as soon as I was able, I would need to go back to the house and make a positive identification before the body can be removed. He asked, "Ms. Grant do you think you'll be able to make a positive id? I was smiling as the devil was dead and killed himself!

After everything I just heard I still wanted to see my daughter. If Dillon was dead there was no need to hurry and identify the body.

The detective continued talking about Dillon. He informed me during their investigation of my home, in addition to finding the weapon next to the body was a half box of bullets. In my attic they found four more weapons with the serial numbers removed, four full boxes of teflon coated bullets, several passports with his picture but different last names in a brief case and a very large sum of cash all which has been taken to the police station and marked as evidence.

He then asked, "Ms. Grant did you know about any of those items?" I replied, "No." And looked over at Phoenix in disbelief and thinking how could all this have happened under my roof and me not know?

I didn't shed a tear for Dillon. I was thinking of the attic. In all the years I've lived in that house I never used the attic, forgot it was there and only seen it once and that was when I moved in. Dillon found the attic and used it for storage of destruction. He was going to kill both of us, change his identify and disappear.

A few minutes later I said, "I want to go see my daughter. If Dillon is dead, he isn't going anywhere. **NOW SOMEONE TAKE ME TO MY DAUGHTER!"**

Now that I had everyone in my room attention, the doctor said, "Ms. Grant I'm sorry we can't release you in the condition you're in."

I assured the doctor I want hold them accountable should something happen to me. I'll sign whatever papers needed for my release but I'm going and you can't stop me.

In case no one believe that I was leaving, I pulled out the IV without knowing what I was doing and blood was gushing. I remove the heart monitor and the machine was going off. I was in pain but kept doing what was needed. I remembered the fall so I ask Phoenix to help me down.

I was in hospital scrubs and the socks given to patients. When I reach the door, the nurses brought a wheel chair and papers for me to sign. Ignoring the wheel chair, I took the papers. I looked at my hands and they were so swollen I couldn't sign my name so I put an X for my signature and had Phoenix witnessed.

--------- ·⬩⬩⬩⬩⬩· ---------

As we were leaving the hospital the doctor explained again about my condition, as if I didn't hear him the first time. I knew the risk I was taking and because of the meds I have been given, my body was weak and I was very tired. But it was time to go and see my daughter.

Phoenix car was in the emergency parking lot and she ask me to stand by the wall while she gets the car. As Phoenix was helping me into her car, the detective caught up with us and said, "The police that was station outside my room would escort us to where Sky was taken and that he would be over later to take our statements."

Just knowing Sky was in some Trauma Center in the city, I was so grateful for the detective and the escort, I found myself crying and thanking God.

On the ride to the Trauma Center my pain had become unbearable but I was determined more than ever to see my daughter so I said nothing to Phoenix not even a moan. I just wanted to keep moving.

I know if she was taken to a Trauma Center the injuries, she sustains were bad. I wouldn't let myself think the worst.

CHAPTER TWENTY-EIGHT

⚜

IT SEEMS LIKE hours had passed since we left Emergency Care. Although we had a police escort and didn't have to stop at traffic lights or stop signs, it seems like the distance between hospitals was too long.

Finally, we made it to the Trauma Center. Once we arrive there was a nurse outside with a wheel chair for me. I guess someone from Emergency Care had phone ahead to let them know we were coming. I accepted the wheel chair and was taken to the floor where Sky was being treated.

Once we arrived on the floor, there seem to be a lot of policeman standing outside her room. A lot of activity going on in her room. Everyone moving very fast and not talking. The only talking I actually heard was from the room where Sky was being treated.

A doctor came and ask if I was related to the young lady that was brought in tonight? I replied, "Yes. I'm, her mother." She asks me to wait outside the room, ask a nurse to bring a chair and bottles of water.

I had so many questions but knew I would have to wait. She went to speak to the police officer and the other doctor that were now standing in the door way.

The Doctor and a Chaplin approached Phoenix and myself. Phoenix grabbed my hand and, in a whisper, ask me not to think the worse.

Too late. I had buried a husband a few years back and knew that seeing a Chaplain in any situation was bad news.

I didn't notice the police officer with them until I heard her asking questions, "May I have your name? Who was I to the lady in the room? What's the address? And how did she know the deceased?"

I answered all questions but one. How did she know the deceased? Because I didn't answer, the officer said she would come back later.

I asked, "If I could please go and be with my daughter?" Everyone stepped aside as I pushed myself out of the wheel chair, holding my side and proceed the walk into her room with my sister and the Chaplain following close behind.

Upon entering the room, the curtains were drawn around the bed and I could hear voices talking about "this patient."

When I move the curtain neither I nor Phoenix was prepared for what we saw. There was Sky lying in bed unconscious, or so I thought, with the right side of her face showing. The left side was bandage up. I ask the doctor to remove the bandages so I could see my baby face. What I saw made me scream until I felt a needle prick in my arm and then blackness.

When I woke up it seem as though I had been dreaming until I realize I was in a hospital. And Sky was in the next bed laying perfectly still. Phoenix crying again.

The doctor came in and explained when your daughter arrived, she was barely alive. She had coded twice in the ambulance and once in the Trauma Center.

Because of the severity of her injuries, they induce her into a coma.

As I lay their weeping, feeling completely numb he explain, the left side of her face will have to be reconstructed as all the bones had been broken along with her nose, her eye had been dislocated and sunk into her head and she has a punctured lung. The tube I saw was draining blood that had built up inside and around her lungs. They were concern about her back as they believe she might have a spinal injury therefore they placed her in a full body brace.

The tube in her mouth was helping her to breath. She continued to explain they needed to insert two IV bags one in each of her arm. Now they would have to wait and see.

Hot tears were running down my face as she explains in great detail what would be taken place over the next few weeks to repair the damage and that full recover time would be at least two years.

I could her talking as though in a whisper. The clock on the wall was the loudest I had ever heard. I focus on the clock to drown out all she was telling me about Sky.

Tick Tock
Tick Tock
Tick Tock

This can't be happening. Wake up Fiona. Wake up!

I looked around and the Chaplain was speaking to me about her faith then darkness came for me.

I woke and looked to my right and no Sky. I was alone in the room except for Phoenix, Casper, La 'niece (her godmother) and Melanie her go to person since she was ten. Phoenix must have called them and explain as much as she could.

My only concern was where in the hell was Sky?

A nurse was trying to change my bandages and I couldn't remember ever getting or having bandages put on except for my eye. Now my arm was in a cast. So, what was she doing?

I asked about Sky and the nurse replied, "She had been taken down to x-ray and would be back shortly." I attempted to get out of bed and she insisted she bring in a wheel chair.

Before Sky return to the room, I requested if they could remove the other bed and bring four chairs. I looked at the nurse, smile and said, "I'm here for the duration even if it meant sitting in this wheel chair." I was silently praying that my pain would ease up soon.

Once the bed was removed everyone took a chair and decided they would wait a while at least till Sky return from taken x-rays. The memory of what happen and why we're both here just made me angry all over again. Then I said, "Dillon tried to kill us."

I heard a voice in my head say, "It could have been worse. You could have been shot in the garage where you might not have been found and he had gotten away." I nodded my head as if in agreement and thank the Lord for watching over us.

Another set of doctors came in later that day to examine Sky but said nothing to me.

A nurse came into the room with red folder with a lot of papers for me to read and sign. After reading all the papers, I sign all the papers except one. The one that read to take her off life support should it be needed.

In another folder was the paper work from Emergency Care for me. I read all the paper work but sign nothing. I knew my injuries as they were already explained to me in great detail in the emergency ward. But my injuries would have to wait. Sky was the priority now. I return the folder to her with none of the paper work sign.

CHAPTER TWENTY-NINE

$$\clubsuit$$

THAT EVENING AROUND eight pm the same detective that was at the hospital with me came to the Trauma Center. He said, "I'm sorry Ms. Grant for what you and your daughter have been thru but there is still the matter of making a positive ID of the man who killed himself upstairs in the bedroom of your house. The quicker you make the ID the sooner you will be able to return to your daughter. The sooner the body can be removed."

Phoenix and the other ladies said they would stay at the hospital with Sky while I went with the detective.

Casper volunteered to go with me back to the house. As we were getting in the back of the police car, I was thinking what a nightmare since this all happen.

When we turn the corner on my street, you would have thought a funeral had taken place and folks were there for the repast.

Police cars lined the streets, news crew, yellow tape blocking the sidewalk and across the entrance of what was once my front door. My entire front yard was taped off and it went half way down the street to where the two guys were.

My front door had heavy plastic hanging down and my front windows had boards nailed on them. Some nice nasty person wrote MURDER HOUSE in black paint on my garage door.

Before getting out the police car I was handed a blanket. I inquired what I needed it. The officer replied that I might want to shield my face from the news crew as this is an active investigation.

There were two policeman doing crowd control so we could get to the front door. As we got out of the police car a microphone was pushed in my face. Casper took the blanket and threw over my head, put his arms around me guiding me down the walk way and into the house.

I never notice the Coroner out there until Marvin whisper it to me. I never turn around as I didn't care. I just wanted this to be over and get back to the Trauma Center.

When I got into the house I turned around and looked down at the street. Other than the news vans, there were so many people standing around looking, watching and sitting in lawn chairs. It's was like a circus and all that's missing is someone selling popcorn.

As I was looking at the people, I saw a few familiar faces and wanted to scream *where were you when all this was going on?* I heard laughter and immediately recognize the men that were standing and pointing that night.

When I step away from the door, I noticed all the blood on the hardwood floor, carpet and walls. The broken mirrors, more blood, the table that was on the floor with three legs and the infamous phone cord.

Going toward the stairs I noticed blood on the banister and shattered glass from the mirror at the bottom of the stairs. *Why didn't I notice this when I first got in the house? I guess you see only what you want.*

Looking into the bedroom where I first saw Sky laying on the floor, tears started down my face. There was so much blood. My face became hot as I pictured Dillon beating and kicking her as she laid there. I kept looking into the room and saw the closet mirrors shattered to pieces, the corner of the night stand with blood on it and then the broken lamp. Self-consciously I touch the top of my head and pulled my hand away quickly as though it was on fire.

Walking down the hallway was more blood on the carpet, cabinets and walls.

Then I saw the bedroom at the end of hall with heavy plastic hanging and yellow tape across the door way with an officer standing in front . When we approached, the officer moves the plastic aside. The detective went in first then Casper. I didn't want to go but Casper held out his hand and said, "It's alright. He can't hurt you anymore."

My legs wouldn't move. Finally, I took hold of his hand and went in with my eye closed. Thanks to Dillon that's all I had for now, one eye. Slowly I open my eye, gasp and held my chest.

There was a person in the corner of room with the word CORONOR on the back of the jacket.

There was a body in the corner near the window sitting upright in a chair covered up. Someone said ready? I said, "Yes". The cover was removed and I just stared. I couldn't move or speak, just stare.

The detective looking at me directly said, "Ms. Grant would you like some water?" I shook my head no. Then in a stern professional voice, "Ms. Grant can you identify the body in this bedroom?"

"Yes, that's Dillon Mason."

He asks how could I be sure considering half the face was gone. I looked directly at him and in a calm voice, "The half I can see has a mark on his face that I put there during the struggle, the bruise knuckles were used to beat Sky and myself and by the shoes he has on."

The stomping and kicking Fiona shoes. That was Dillon for sure. The Devil was dead.

After the identification was made, Dillon was removed from the house, I ask the detective if I could say for a few more minutes to obsess the damage that had taken place. Each room had been completed destroyed. My entire house looked like it belonged to someone that was moving out instead of actually living here. I learn from the detective the destruction I was seeing was done by the police as this was now a crime scene.

CHAPTER THIRTY

TRAUMA CENTER.

Phoenix started calling our immediate family telling them what had taken place at my house and where we were. Eventually everyone showed and was in disbelief of what Dillon had done.

Day four.

Sky being in the hospital and in a induce coma, I called Jasper and some of her long-forgotten friends. Since Jasper lived so far away, he was the last to arrive but stayed the entire time with me at the hospital. Her friends had come and left but promise to return soon.

I left a list of names at the nurses' station that only the following people are to go into her room.

Day five.

A doctor and same Chaplain came into the room. Seeing them again together I didn't like it but was prepared. The doctor approached and asked, "Is there anyone you want to call, now would be the time."

Jasper and I stood up together, I looked at the doctor and the Chaplain. In a calm voice, "I've already called on my Heavenly Father." The Chaplain smile and nodded. As they both walked away...I kept saying she's still here and alive.

Family and friends in the waiting room starting crying as they heard what the doctor had said. No tears from me. In a calm voice, I told everyone to stop crying and not give up on Sky. As of this moment she's alive. Just pray. I have not given up and I want until I have to let her go. Until then we all should pray.

While Jasper was sitting with Sky, I would visit the Chapel and sit for hours. My dad would often time come and sit assuring me not to worry. She's in GOD hands. She's strong and you have enough faith for both of you. (My child was not going to die).

Later that afternoon a doctor and nurse came into the room and reminded me of my injuries. Although I was starting to feel pain more and more, I wouldn't let them treat me, not as long as Sky was in a coma. I could endure the pain. The pain I felt would have to wait until the doctor or doctors come up with a plan of treatment for my child.

Day nine.

The doctor came with good news. Still in an induce coma, her vital signs had improved significantly and they could go ahead and talk about surgeries that she would need. I smiled and looked up and whispered, *"Thank You Abba."*

Later that day a plastic surgeon was brought in to discuss her case and explain what would be taking place over the next few weeks. I gave the only picture I had and said make her look like this again. He looks at me and said, "I will do by best."

Day ten.

An Ophthalmologist came and said it was a possibility they could save her eye.

Day thirteen.

The plastic surgeon came again and informed me they were going to insert titanium plates under the skin to reconstruct her face and to keep her eye in place, also they were going to repair her nose.

I was informed it would be best if all the surgeries where perform while she was in a coma and let the healing start before bringing her out as the pain would be significant.

By this time, I told Phoenix to take dad home and if she was coming back to stop and buy me some clothes. I was not leaving the hospital without Sky, if at all possible. Since Jasper came straight from the airport to the hospital, he had his suitcase with him and stayed at the Trauma Center with me.

After they left only Jasper and I remained at the Trauma Center. Together we both prayed.

I was in so much pain that I could no longer feel anything but knew eventually I would have to be treated and soon.

Day fourteen.

The tube from her side was remove and a large clear bandage had been place over the hole.

The next surgery would be to craft skin from her thigh to cover the hole where the tube had been inserted .

Day twenty.

The doctor had completed all the surgeries and in five days they would bring her out of the coma. She would be heavily sedated and hardly feel pain.

Day twenty-six.

She moaned.

Jasper immediately went to get a nurse. The nurse entered the room with a doctor close behind. While examining her, she opens her eye as half her face was still covered by bandages. The doctor reported she looked fine but would run some test just to be sure.

Sky continued to look around the room. She didn't know where she was or what had happened. Because of the breathing tube down her throat she was unable to speak. We were told it would have to remain there until her breathing became normal.

Both Jasper and I were crying and laughing. She was awake and alive. Jaspers whispered, "Moms her breath smells minty." I looked at him and smiled.

Later that evening I went to wash up in the restroom and for the first time I actually looked in a mirror at myself. I know why the hospital staff was worried. My face was scared, I'm wearing an eye patch and had no hair in the top of my head.

The pain became great until I had no choice but to seek emergency treatment. I felt comfortable with Jasper to stay with Sky so I had Phoenix take me to the hospital where my doctor was located. *But that's another story for another time.*

My Sky was awake! She was alive!

Now the hard part. Telling her about Dillon. I called everyone and let them know Sky was awake but not ready to receive visitors or phone calls. Phoenix, Casper, La 'niece and Melanie came anyway.

Day twenty-eight.

The tube had been removed from her throat.

The detective was back and wanted to speak with Sky. We stepped in the hallway and I informed him the doctor suggested we wait until a Psychiatrist was present before telling her of Dillon demise.

I was also thinking what her reaction would be when I told her I had him cremated.

In the presence of the doctor, Psychiatrist, nurse, and Jasper, I told her about Dillon and how he took his own life. She just looked at me. Then at each person in the room then back at me.

I saw the tear and reached out to her. To my surprise, she slapped my hand away and started screaming get out. Get out! Everyone left the room except the doctor, Jasper and myself. Sky had to be sedated and finally sleep came.

The Psychiatrist came back later that afternoon and spoke with Sky and ask if she understood what was said earlier. Sky whispered, "Yes". The Psychiatrist left but not before saying she would need therapy to help her get pass this dramatic experience.

Later that evening Sky asked why did Dillon kill himself?" I replied, "He was a coward and took the easy way out." Her response did not surprise me, "No. You're wrong. He was not a coward. He loved me."

I looked long and hard at Sky and asked, "Do you know what happen to you? To me? Do you know why you are in the hospital and I look like this?" I handed her my compact mirror so she could see herself. She said nothing but cried. I wanted to comfort her but thought against it. I explained to her what all had taken place at the house, the shooting, how he shot innocent people, the surgeries she had, the number of days she's been at the Trauma Center.

Jasper came into the room and wanted to be by her side, to comfort her. I said, "No, she needs to cry, scream whatever it took to get those emotions out."

I ask Jasper to get me a cup of coffee and I would join him in the waiting room so Sky could be alone with her thoughts about all she's been told.

A few hours later, Casper showed up with food and bottle water for Jasper and myself. He also thought to bring me a thermal for coffee.

An hour later I went back to sit with Sky while she slept. The doctor came into the room and I asked, "Why she couldn't remember?" He informed me she may have temporary memory lost.

A few days later the detective was back. This time asking Sky questions about Dillon, about the guns, numerous passports in different names and satchel of money found in the attic." This line of questions confused her more. She could only shake her head and replied, "I don't know."

Day thirty-two.

Sky was released from the hospital. We had no place to go as the police still had the yellow tape across the door and informed me it was still a crime scene. He suggested the names of companies that clean up crime scenes and are paid by the city in which the crime occurred.

Until it happens to me, I never knew companies like exist in real life.

CHAPTER THIRTY-ONE

✤

I PHONE CASPER and inquired if he knew where we should go. He suggested we head north for a few days and contact my insurance company as they would provide us a place to stay until my house was ready to move back into.

Six months later we're moving back into the house. Most of the furniture was gone, new carpet was put in and money from insurance company was in the mail.

————— ✦✦✦✦✦ —————

Just being back in that house which I no longer consider my home has had a horrific effect on me more than it did to Sky. Probably because of her memory lost.

Nevertheless, just being back where that dreadful night of horror started has not been healthy situation for either of us.

There are times I hear Sky crying or having a nightmare. Some nights we both have nightmares and I'm sure about the same thing.

Immediately after moving back into the house Sky and I both went to therapy. It has been a dramatic experience, for both of us, sharing our inner thoughts with strangers. I want to believe it has help. But deep down I feel it isn't helping fast enough.

I know Sky mind and body has gone thru all stages of grief. But thank God she is not in a state of depression.

I've been diagnosed with sever PTSD (up till that night I never heard of PTSD) and clinical depression. I must say the depression started when I checked my retirement funds and it had a balance of $17.82 The monies found in the attic was mine as it was the exact amount missing. Unfortunately, it's now considered evidence. *(another story for another time)*

She still has questions I don't answer. I feel has her mom, the answers I give here would only hurt and serve no real purpose. But as his wife she has a right to ask. Maybe one day the questions will stop. She was hurt from the inside out as this was her first experience in losing a love one. Even if it was Dillon.

Even today she looks sad and cries a lot. I ask no questions. I told her once when you cry it signifies that you are alive, it helps cleanse the soul and GOD has shown you favor.

The only way I know to help my child is to be there and listen. Give advice when needed and talk when she is ready. I keep reassuring her that what happened is not her fault. For anybody to do what he did took some planning of hatred and was pure evil.

After I met Dillon, been around him I always felt a chill. I knew and could feel something was amiss but never would have expect this to happen. Never in a million years did I want to be right about having the devil in the bedroom.

Honor Your Past

And

Treasure What You Have Now

CHAPTER THIRTY-TWO

IT'S TOO LATE to undo what Dillon has done. All we can do is move forward and hope for the best.

It's what I call one of life many lessons.

Failure or quitting is not an option for Sky or myself, we continue to strive forward, hope for the best, stay in prayer and faith.

It's been five years since that tragic event in our lives. I constantly remind both of us we're still here.

Sky is still a beautiful young woman with a beautiful spirit. She's put her designer clothes, jewelry and furs in various consignment stores and with the monies she received, return back to school working on her degree and purchased a car.

Jasper is still around and back in her life.

Now this one, *Jasper Singleton*, I've always approved of and one day hope when all is well with her, they plan to move forward and make a life together. Maybe somewhere tropical so mom can visit.

Casper is still with me and I'm thinking of accepting his offer of marriage. Move to another state where we can sit and look upon beautiful greenery and watch our horses grazing in the grass.

It's taken me longer to get over the tragedy of that one night. I'm still in therapy and working on designing a blue print for my life. I know it's going to take time but I'm getting there, fore now I wear a robe on Sundays and preach HIS Word.

ACKNOWLEDGMENT

To GOD for not allowing us to look forward and back on that night.

To my daughter, Sky for being brave. For having the will to survive the tragedy and lost. To not let what happen determine or define who she is and what she can become. You made up your mind what you wanted out of life, went for and achieved it. I'm so very proud of you, Sky. Watching you smile helps remind me that life can be beautiful if you look within yourself.

Jasper, my dear sweet son, thanks for dropping everything to be here for Sky. You never talked about it, but I know you quite your job to be with us, just as I know you had another life and gave it all up just to be near Sky and I love you for it. I'll never forget what you said… moms she's in a coma but her breath is minty fresh.

To my sister, Phoenix for being there and never wavering. You'll always be my person no matter what. Thanks for taking over when I couldn't and the numerous calls you made. You did a great job of taking care of me when I needed you.

To La 'niece and Melanie for being my prayer warriors and looking after us both when I could no longer stand alone fight this battle by myself. You left your place of business, your clients and came to sit by our side for days on end. The only question you ask was where is the Dillon. After that you took both our hands and never let go. You'll forever remain in my heart. I love you both.

Casper from the day we meet you said, "You would never leave me" and you've proven yourself to be true. You came into my life unexpectedly and I'm so glad you did. And yes, you are still adorable and I treasure our friendship forever and always. If you ask me again, I'll say yes to being Mrs. Casper Grant Dupont.

Before that terrible night I thought I knew how to pray but I didn't. I've learned to humble myself before the Lord for given Sky and myself a second chance at life. I daily give praise to the LORD for showing me how use and understand motherly instincts, not let go and trust my judgement.

And to you Dillon may you rest in hell where your soul is tormented. If you had not been so evil, I would not know how strong my faith, belief and my own strength as a mother